A
STROKE OF
MISFORTUNE

NANCY GOTTER GATES

SILVER DAGGER
M Y S T E R I E S
An Imprint of The Overmountain Press
JOHNSON CITY, TENNESSEE

This book is a work of fiction. All names, characters, places, and events are either the product of the author's imagination or are used fictitiously. Any resemblance to actual events or persons, living or dead, is entirely coincidental and beyond the intent of either the author or the publisher.

Book design by Cherisse McGinty

Hardcover ISBN 1-57072-296-X
Trade Paper ISBN 1-57072-267-8
Copyright © 2005 by Nancy Gotter Gates
Printed in the United States of America
All Rights Reserved

1 2 3 4 5 6 7 8 9 0

TAKE A STAB AT THESE MYSTERIES
COMING
SOON

Bitsy heads to Amelia Island, Florida, to visit her friends Garrett and Ellie, but she quickly finds herself battling Ernie, the neighborhood bully. After overhearing a sinister plan, the kids team up with Ernie and his twin sister, Bernie, to investigate dark secrets in a nearby abandoned house. Could one of those secrets be a ghost?

Bitsy and the Mystery at Amelia Island

by Vonda Skinner Skelton

Death by Any Other Name

by Ellis Vidler

If Williamsburg shop owner Emma Spencer wants to live, she has to find out why someone wants her dead. Her investigation ranges from the swamps of South Carolina to a deserted farm in Virginia, and Emma uncovers more than anyone expected: family secrets, an old murder, and deadly connections.

SILVER DAGGER MYSTERIES

WOULD YOU LIKE TO WRITE A REVIEW OF A SILVER DAGGER MYSTERY? VISIT OUR WEB SITE FOR DETAILS

www.silverdaggermysteries.com

ALL SILVER DAGGER MYSTERIES ARE AVAILABLE IN BOTH TRADE PAPER AND HARDCOVER AT YOUR LOCAL BOOKSTORE OR DIRECTLY FROM THE PUBLISHER
P.O. Box 1261 • Johnson City, TN 37605
1-800-992-2691

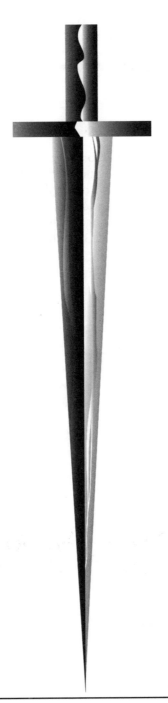

www.nancygottergates.com

For Karen, George, Robert, and Margery

ACKNOWLEDGMENTS

The past and present members of my writing group all gave me invaluable advice and suggestions, and I could never have completed this book without their astute comments and observations: Diane Berry, Carla Buckley, Helen Goodman, Wendy Greene, Ellen Hunter, Dorothy O'Neill, and my dear friend who passed away, Charlotte Perkins. Detective Sam Jones of the Greensboro (North Carolina) Police Department helped me get the bomb scene right. I'd also like to thank my editor, Sherry Lewis, for her sharp eye and quick pen.

PROLOGUE

GERALDINE STAPLETON HUGGED ME IN HER BEEFY ARMS AND ROCKED me like a baby. "You're going to be mad as hell, but don't feel guilty about that. It's a normal reaction. Part of the process."

She stepped back and looked me in the eye. Her red hair gleamed in the dying sunlight that streamed through my living room window, and her abundant makeup made her aging face look even older. I didn't know her well—I'd only spoken to her casually in the hall at La Hacienda—but she and her husband, Phil, were the first to appear at my door when I returned from the hospital.

"Now, hon," Phil said, touching her gently on the arm, "don't upset her." His almost incandescent white hair and Norman Rockwell-like features were in sharp contrast to her flamboyance.

"She's already upset." Geraldine brushed him off. "I just want to assure her it's okay."

"I'm fine," I lied, hoping they'd go away. I wanted to crawl into bed and sleep for a year. The last thing I wanted to do was entertain guests. Every inch of me was numb, exhausted.

As I started to back away from the door, assuming they'd leave, they stepped into the room. Phil, I now noticed, was carrying a bag from KFC.

"We brought you some dinner," Geraldine said. She turned to her husband. "Would you make her some coffee to go with it?"

She pulled me toward the couch as he went to the kitchen. He'd never been in my home, but all condos in our building are identical. They lived two floors down.

She plopped down beside me on my yellow-striped couch. "Of course you're not fine," she said.

I stared silently out at the Gulf, where the setting sun had made a blood-red trail on the water.

"You just haven't had time to feel anything yet," she said. "When someone dies that suddenly, you're not prepared."

I envisioned Paul's smiling face as he kissed me before going out for his early morning jog. For a moment, I felt seized by such unbearable sorrow, I thought I couldn't endure it. Then numbness washed over me again. "He was only fifty-nine," I murmured, "just two years older than me. He was so excited about living on the beach."

"You haven't been in Sarasota long, have you?" she asked, patting my hand sympathetically.

"Six months."

For the first time, I realized how alone I was. My only child, Mark, lived in Toledo, and most of my friends were in Columbus. How could I cope? I hugged myself to keep from visibly trembling.

"Fifty-nine *is* young," Geraldine said reflectively. "Did he have heart disease?"

"Not that we knew."

She took my hand in hers. "Like I said, Emma, you'll be numb for a while, then you'll be mad at Paul for dying and leaving you. That's when I want you to come to me and let it all hang out. You'll feel a whole lot better if you do."

Phil came out of the kitchen, carrying my tole tray, and set it on the coffee table in front of me. The tray held a plate of fried chicken and fries, a side dish of slaw, and a cup of coffee that looked way too strong. I could tell from the stray grains on the saucer, he'd used my instant. "This will make you feel better," he said, his tone as benevolent as a preacher's.

Stifling my urge to say *I doubt it*, I tried to smile. "Thanks."

"We should go now, sweetheart," Phil said to Geraldine.

"Do eat," she said to me. "You need to take care of yourself." What she left unsaid was that there was no one else to do it now.

She engulfed me again in a generous hug, and suddenly I let go, weeping with such intensity, I could hardly catch my breath. She held me tightly until my tears were exhausted. Her florid looks and distressing candor were forgotten, and I drew strength from her compassion. Gerry, as I would come to know, was a parcel of unusual human kindness, done up in garish wrappings as though it were camouflage.

From that moment, our relationship blossomed into a strong, enduring friendship over the next nine months, fostered by her ability to guide me through the unforeseen complexities of grief. Her straightforward, no-nonsense manner was surprisingly healing, especially when I felt the rage she'd predicted.

"Go ahead, tell him what a son of a bitch he was to leave you," she'd say. "Now that he can't answer you back, you can say just about any damned thing you please. Get it out of your system."

Sometimes I'd go to her crying then end up laughing at some outrageous remark. Not everyone reacted to Gerry that way. Some found her too blunt, too outspoken. But I loved her for her uncompromising honesty. What you saw was what you got. There wasn't an ounce of pretense in her.

She and Phil had served as informal ombudsmen for the folks at La Hacienda almost since they first moved in. She was a natural leader; Phil loved to help, too, in his own quiet way.

As I got stronger, they began to ask for my help when someone complained to them that there was litter on our beach or people weren't parking where they were supposed to. I'm sure Gerry knew I had a strong desire to be needed and useful.

Becoming involved was an important part of my healing process. We'd even get called upon for personal problems when a neighbor had no family close by.

"Mona Sapstein got screwed by the plumber who fixed her toilet," Gerry would call me to report. "She's so frail, she's just not up to fighting with them. Let's go talk turkey to those guys. What do you say?" And we'd drive to their headquarters and get it straightened out.

Without Gerry and Phil, my pilgrimage through grief would have been more difficult. When tragedy befell them, I was ready to go to the ends of the earth to help. What I didn't know was how my involvement would put me in extreme danger.

CHAPTER · 1

WHEN THERE ARE TWELVE FLOORS OF RETIREES, A DEATH NOW AND then is to be expected. But when two residents of La Hacienda passed away two days apart in early October, we all were confronted with our own precarious mortality. With more than two-thirds of the occupants yet to return from their second homes up North, the building was relatively empty. It brought us up short.

Ninety-three-year-old Spencer Brower died first. Since he'd been in poor health for some months, we'd anticipated his demise. We were saddened but not surprised.

Geraldine Stapleton's death, on the other hand, shocked everyone. She'd just been diagnosed with chronic leukemia and was undergoing treatment in the hospital. Phil had told me her prognosis was good. According to him, the doctor said she would probably live at least another ten or more years.

She'd been in the hospital almost two weeks when I got a phone call from Mickey, their next-door neighbor on the ninth floor. "Emma," she said, "Gerry died unexpectedly early this morning. I thought you'd want to know."

I nearly dropped the phone. Geraldine had always seemed so indestructible that it hadn't occurred to me she was in any danger of dying so soon. "I can't believe it! I thought she was doing well."

"They don't know what happened. I suppose it could have been a heart attack."

There hadn't been time yet to make funeral arrangements, Mickey told me, and we talked about how devastating it would be for Phil. When I hung up, I decided to fix something for his dinner and take it down to him, thinking of how they'd brought me food when Paul died nine months earlier.

I called his number twice before I found him home. I'm sure he'd been at the undertaker's. I knew the drill from my own grim experience.

After we hung up, I went downstairs to take a casserole to him. When he opened his door, I hardly recognized him. His face was drawn and haggard, his complexion pale, and the sadness in his eyes almost unbearable to see. Gerry was the strong one of the two, and though Phil is a delightful man, he always deferred to his wife. I wondered how he would manage without her.

"I'm so sorry, Phil." That seemed so inane, but I didn't know what else to say. I took his hand in mine, hugging my dinner offering in my left arm. His hand felt like ice. I nodded toward the casserole. "Let me put this in the refrigerator for you."

When I came back from the kitchen, he was sitting bent over on the sofa, his face in his hands, weeping silently. I sat down in a chair and waited quietly as he pulled himself together. I wasn't quite sure whether to leave or stay, but I wanted to find out what I could do to help.

He pulled a handkerchief from his cardigan pocket and wiped his face. "Forgive me. But I can't seem to deal with this."

My curiosity about the cause of Gerry's untimely death had been growing since I'd learned of it, and I'd planned to ask him some questions. But his grief had so overwhelmed him, I thought better of it and decided to wait till later. However, I did want to say something that might help assuage his sorrow.

"Remember what Gerry said to me when Paul died?" I didn't know if Gerry's brusque style would work with Phil, but I decided to try it. After all, he'd lived with her outspokenness for forty-five years. It might be just what he needed.

He looked at me blankly.

"She said I'd be mad at Paul for dying on me, but that was a normal reaction."

"Oh, yes," he said softly. "I remember now. But I couldn't be mad at Gerry. Never could be. I know she made some people angry. But not me. I loved her with all my heart. Maybe I'm mad at God for taking her."

Uh-oh. I'd gotten myself in hot water now. "I know what you mean, Phil. But I think these things just happen. Surely God isn't sitting up there, pointing at us and saying, 'Okay, buddy, it's your turn.' Why would he want to take Gerry? Or Paul? Or little babies, for that matter? We just have to accept it and go on."

"I hope I can."

"I'm here at any time to help you, the way you and Gerry helped me."

"I appreciate that." His attempt at a smile failed miserably.

"What can I do for you, Phil? Is there anyone I can call?"

"My daughter's flying in from Pittsburgh. She'll know who to call, what to do."

"Why don't you let me pick her up at the airport?"

"Thanks, Emma," he sighed. "She gets in around six on . . . let me think . . . I'm pretty sure it's US Airways."

"What's her last name? I can only think of Arlene. Remember, I haven't met her yet. Can you describe her, so I'll recognize her?"

"Arlene Caviness. She's forty-two, not too tall, and she's thin. She has kind of reddish hair like her mom." At the mention of Geraldine, his eyes closed again, and tears ran unimpeded down his cheeks. His shoulders shook with silent sobs.

He needed to be alone. I could probably be of more help once his daughter arrived.

I stood up to go. "Perhaps Arlene will think of some things I can do for you."

He started to rise from the sofa, then suddenly crumpled and fell to the floor. For a moment, I was too shocked to move. I couldn't believe something terrible was happening to Phil too. Pulling myself together, I knelt beside him, but he was incoherent, making strange sounds, and as limp as a pile of rags.

I rushed to the kitchen, where there was a wall phone, and called 911. Assured the paramedics were on their way, I hurried back to Phil, taking an afghan from the back of the sofa to cover him. Sitting on the floor beside him, I put my hand on his slack one and kept reassuring him he'd be all right, though in my heart, I felt it was a lie. What was happening to this family?

The emergency personnel came tumbling through the door within ten minutes. As they worked over Phil, visions of Paul's lifeless form lying on the beach, flopping like a puppet on strings as they tried to shock his heart back into beating, nearly overwhelmed me. Bile rose in my throat, and I had to momentarily turn my back to try to shut out the sight. It was useless. The emotions I'd tried so hard to suppress over the past months threatened to paralyze me, but I knew I had to be strong for Phil. I couldn't let him down now.

When they loaded him on a gurney and prepared to take him to the ambulance, I asked if I could go along.

"You can meet us at the hospital," one of them told me. "We don't have room for you to ride with us."

Out in the hall, my heart sank as I watched them roll Phil's inert body into the elevator. After heading upstairs to my own condo on the eleventh floor, I gathered up my purse to leave, then realized it was nearly time to pick up Arlene. I decided to get her first, knowing it would be upsetting to arrive in Sarasota and not have anyone meet her.

The airport is on the far north side of the city, and I live near the south bridge on Siesta Key. I drove out of La Hacienda's parking lot in my silver Civic hatchback and up Midnight Pass Road, toward the north bridge, which crosses the Intracoastal Waterway. I passed the long row of high-rises, which obscure beautiful Crescent Beach and its sugar-white sand, and for the zillionth time felt a stab of guilt for living in one of them.

Intellectually I know the rampant building along our beaches is not a good thing. On the other hand, I love looking out at the Gulf, and the high-rises are my only affordable option.

I wondered if living here would be the same without Gerry. A sudden, delayed fit of grief overwhelmed me, and I could barely see the road through my tears.

With traffic what it is, particularly in late afternoon, I wasn't any too early to meet Arlene. Just before I left home, I'd scribbled her name on a sign, figuring that was an easier way to identify her.

The red hair tipped me off, and the fact that she was obviously looking for someone. I held up my sign, and she approached me.

"Arlene? I'm Emma Daniels. Friend of your mom and dad. I'm so very sorry for your loss." I'm sure my eyes were so red, she couldn't doubt my sincerity.

"Thanks," she said softly.

She was a thin, sad woman. I'd guess she once was pretty, but now everything seemed to come to points—pointed chin, pointed nose, sharp cheekbones. Extreme slenderness might be considered attractive in young women, but as one ages, anorexic bodies take on a cadaverous quality.

"Where's Dad?" she asked.

I'd dreaded this moment. I tried to make it as benign as I could. After all, Phil might have completely recovered by now, although that seemed unlikely. "He became ill while I was visiting with him. They've taken him to the hospital, and I'm going to take you there."

For a minute she turned so pale, I thought she was going to faint. But she recovered quickly.

"I was in such a rush to get here," she said, "I packed only a carry-on. So I don't have to go to baggage claim."

I could tell she was going to be far more stoic than her father. That was good. Someone in the family needed to be in charge.

Phil was still in the emergency room when we arrived at the hospital. They let Arlene see him, while I sat in the waiting room and tried to read months-old magazines to keep from imagining the worst.

When she returned, she flopped into the chair beside me, looking drained, and closed her eyes.

I waited till she opened them again. "How's your dad?" I asked, fearing what the answer might be.

"He had a massive stroke. His right side is paralyzed and he's lost his speech."

"Oh, no, Arlene." I reached over to embrace her. How much more could this family endure?

I offered to take her to dinner, but she declined, saying she didn't feel like eating. I'd planned to spend the evening with her at the hospital, but she said she wanted to stay with her father in the emergency room till they could get him a room upstairs. She thought I should go on home.

"Will you at least call me when you're ready to leave and let me pick you up?" I asked.

"I appreciate it, but I'll probably spend the night here if I can."

I hunted through my purse for a scrap of paper and wrote down my phone number. "Please call me at any time," I said, giving it to her. "Your mother was so kind when my husband died, I'd like to return the favor."

As I drove home, I thought of what Arlene was up against. I didn't know a whole lot about her except that she was an only child and had once been in an unhappy marriage. Gerry had told me that she'd finally divorced the guy and was struggling to make ends meet on her low-paying job, even though her ex sent her small support payments for their fourteen-year-old daughter.

Whenever I start feeling sorry for myself, I think of someone like Arlene, who lost a husband, not by death, but by mistrust and rejection, and who barely has enough money to make it day to day. Paul and I loved each other deeply, and even though he died at fifty-nine, he'd invested wisely, allowing me to live comfortably.

* * *

When I hadn't heard from Arlene by lunchtime the next day, I decided to pay a visit to the hospital. Arriving at Phil's room, I found him in the far bed by the window, a curtain drawn between him and his sleeping roommate. Phil was dozing, too, his face relaxed in sleep, so the paralysis wasn't evident.

Arlene sat in a chair near the foot of her father's bed, her eyes closed and her chin on her chest. The sound of my footsteps woke her, and she greeted me with a solemn nod of her head. She got up from her chair and bade me to sit down. She stood, her frail body slouched against the windowsill.

"I hope you'll let me take you home to get some rest," I said.

"I don't want to leave him just yet. Maybe later today. Please don't sit around and wait for me to call you. I can catch a cab, and once I'm home, I'll have Dad's car. I have so many things to take care of, like the final arrangements for Mom's service."

Arlene was obviously afraid of imposing on me. Or did she simply want me to butt out? I wasn't sure.

As we talked, a tall, solemn figure appeared in the doorway. I assumed it was an off-duty doctor, since he was dressed in shirt and tie.

"Ms. Caviness?" he asked, looking from one of us to the other. Clearly he did not know which was Arlene.

She stood up straight. "Yes?"

"May I speak with you down the hall please?"

She excused herself and followed him, leaving me to speculate on what it was all about. I hoped it wasn't more bad news.

Fifteen minutes later, Arlene walked into the room alone, her face pallid and slack. Her eyes seemed unfocused, as though unable to accept some horrible truth.

I jumped up and met her halfway into the room. "What happened?"

She put her hand to her mouth and looked at her sleeping father with such profound sorrow, I was sure she'd been told he would die. She looked pointedly at me and walked back into the hall, with the implicit command that I should follow. I caught up with her outside the door and put my arm around her waist to comfort her. Saying nothing, she kept walking till we got to the waiting room. She glanced around to make sure no one could hear us and then gestured for me to sit on the worn Naugahyde couch. She perched on the edge of the cushion beside me and began to massage her temples, as if she suffered from a terrible headache.

"Can you tell me?" I asked gently.

"That was a police detective," she said, her voice shaking.

"A detective?" I was confused.

She clasped her fingers together in her lap and stared at them. "He said the autopsy results were back. Mama didn't die from cancer."

"Did she have a heart attack?" I asked, but I didn't think a detective would be here to tell her that.

"She . . . she was smothered!" Arlene could barely say the words. She closed her eyes in a grimace of anguish, then opened them again and almost whispered, "Like with a pillow."

I sat speechless at this unimaginable turn of events. How could this be?

"And that's not the worst of it." Arlene looked at me. "He thinks Daddy did it."

I was so caught off guard, I grabbed Arlene's arm for support. So the detective *thinks* her father did it! If he didn't know for sure, why would he say such a thing? It was cruel, inhuman. I silently raged at his callousness, then I realized he must have been testing her, gauging her reaction to see if she knew.

"Look, Arlene," I said, taking her shaking hands in my own, trying to will calmness into her frail body, "that was just a fishing expedition. He wanted to know if your father had confided in you any such plans. I'll bet he has no proof at all."

Arlene, who'd been crying softly, nodded her head vigorously in agreement. "My parents were very much in love, always have been. He worshiped the ground she walked on." She said it defiantly, making sure I understood their devotion.

I knew the police were bound to ask her sooner or later, so to prepare her, I tried to put it as gently as possible. "Could he have loved her so very much that he simply couldn't bear to see her suffer?" As soon as the words were out of my mouth, I regretted them. It sounded so much more cruel than I'd meant it to be.

But Arlene didn't appear offended. Assuring me that it was utterly impossible for him to do such a thing, she got up and began to pace back and forth in front of the sofa. "No, no. He's the most gentle man in the world. He couldn't hurt a fly! Besides, he'd told me the doctors had said Mom would probably live a long time, and he was going to surprise her with a trip to Paris when she was through with her chemo."

I had to agree that it made no sense at all. Although I'd known the couple less than a year, I couldn't believe he would take her life, under any circumstances. Their religious beliefs alone would keep him from even thinking about what neither of us had been able to say out loud: mercy killing.

I was convinced that Phil had nothing to do with Geraldine's death. But I did wonder why they'd done an autopsy on her. Something had apparently made them suspicious.

"I can't fathom why they suspect your father, especially if he authorized an autopsy. Do you have any idea why one was done?"

"She'd been on an experimental drug, and the doctors were anxious to see what effect it had. It didn't have to go through the coroner because they had no idea it was a murder."

"And they could tell that it was suffocation?" I asked.

"That's what the detective said," Arlene replied. She'd wiped away her tears, and by the set of her jaw, I could tell she did not intend to break down again. She sat back down, hard, on the sofa and sighed. "Poor Dad."

"What are you going to do?"

"I don't know," she replied morosely. "I have a feeling they're going to watch him like a hawk to see if his health improves enough, so they can throw him in jail. But even in the state he's in, it would be devastating for him to find out they suspect him of such a thing. After all he's been through!"

"Is he capable of understanding what's going on around him?" If Phil couldn't communicate, I wondered if he would be cognizant of his situation.

"Oh, yes, I'm sure of it. I can see it in his eyes. If they openly accuse him, he'll know it. That's what makes it so terrible. My dad is a very sensitive man." She shook her head sorrowfully. "And if his health improves? The doctors say that with therapy he might regain some speech, although they're more optimistic that he'll gain partial control of his arm and leg."

"That's good news."

"But can't you see?" she said plaintively, "if he gets better, he'd probably go to jail if they convicted him. That would kill him."

The irony of the situation was clear: Phil seemed doomed to live in shackles of one kind or another—either the prison of physical disability if he didn't improve, or a jail cell if he did.

That evening, feeling an overwhelming need to hash over Phil and Arlene's plight, I called my friend Cal Murray. I'd met him at a dinner party in the spring, and we'd been seeing each other since. It wasn't exactly a romance—I wasn't ready for anything like that only nine months after Paul's death—but a deepening friendship. Cal's wife had left him more than three years earlier after thirty-some years of marriage, and his pain and sense of abandonment had diminished but not disappeared. Perhaps our friendship was fueled by our mutual sense of loss.

I told him the story as it had unfolded so far.

"What an unbelievable situation," he said. "The poor guy can't defend himself at all."

"And I've realized there's more fallout for Arlene, in addition to the horror of having her father accused of murder. Though I'm sure she hasn't even thought about it. Her dad is her only concern."

"What's that?"

"Geraldine once told me how worried they were about how Arlene would cope after they'd gone. She has few job skills and barely earns enough to make ends meet. They were afraid she could never save anything for retirement."

"I assume they were planning to will her everything."

"Absolutely. But like the rest of us, they were afraid some catastrophic illness might eat up everything they owned. So they tried to protect their assets the best they could. Unfortunately, Phil has had bad health for quite a while, and he didn't qualify for life or long-term-care insurance."

"That's rough." Cal's concern was genuine. He'd told me his father's final illness had almost bankrupted his mother some years earlier.

"It is," I said. "But Geraldine did qualify. They figured if Phil got sick, she could nurse him and keep the costs down. But if she died first, her life insurance would pay for any nursing costs he might have."

"And if he died first, she had long-term-care insurance to cover her expenses."

"Exactly." I never had to spell things out for Cal.

Both of us were silent for a moment, wrapped in thought.

"But now," I continued, "if Phil is suspected in her death, he won't get any of her life insurance money."

There was a pause as Cal took everything in. "Damn, you're right. Murderers can't profit from their grisly deed. And did you realize the cops might think the insurance was part of the motive? Especially since she was the only one who had a policy?"

"Oh, my gosh, I hadn't thought of that. And if he's not well enough to bring to trial, I'm pretty sure he never will get any money from it. Unless there's some proof he didn't do it."

"So how does this affect Arlene?" Cal asked. "That's what you started out to tell me."

"He'll be going into a nursing home, I'm sure. If it's long term, there goes the money—"

"—because he has to spend down all his assets and sell his condo before Medicaid kicks in. And there goes Arlene's inheritance. It sucks, doesn't it?" Cal sounded angry.

"It looks like Arlene will be up the proverbial creek."

"You're right," Cal said. "It's a mess."

"It sure is," I agreed.

The next day I read Geraldine's obituary in the *Herald-Tribune*. Her memorial service was scheduled for one-thirty at Siesta Key Chapel, at the north end of the island.

The intriguingly rustic building sits high above the ground on stilt-like poles, well above any possible tidal surge. Its jungle-like setting, unusual for a place of worship, is in keeping with much of the rest of the island. Masses of live oaks, palms, and Australian pines hover over palmettos and sea grape.

When I arrived, the sanctuary, not surprisingly, was full. The minister could be forgiven his flowery remarks since, for once, they were actually true.

"Geraldine Stapleton loved life and lived it to the fullest," he intoned, short on originality but full of sincerity. "As soon as she and her beloved husband, Phillip, moved to our town, she became involved in the community. She wasn't one who craved the spotlight, but she worked devotedly behind the scenes in many organizations, her only desire to make the world a better place.

"Her compassionate heart was saddened by suffering of any kind, and she set about to right any wrongs that she saw. Her passing is a great loss to all of us, and we shall miss her immensely.

"But today we celebrate her life and her contributions to the enhancement of life in our town. Those whose lives she touched are far richer for the experience. She brought out the best in all who knew her."

"Amen," I said silently.

At the end of the service, Arlene stood at the rear of the sanctuary to speak to each of the mourners, and the long line moved slowly. I had no doubt each one was sharing some special memory of Gerry with Arlene.

As I stood in line, a slim, blonde, middle-aged woman behind me asked, "Did you know Gerry well?"

"Yes, she lived in my condominium."

"She was such a special person."

"How did you know her?" I asked.

"We were in hospice together. She had a special way of relating to dying patients. It's tragic that all her good works were stopped so abruptly. She wasn't expected to die anytime soon, so they hadn't requested hospice services for her. After all she'd given to others, she never had the chance to benefit from it herself."

Her words were an epiphany to me. I'd been so upset about the cops' suspicion of Phil, I'd never once thought that someone else was walking around free and above suspicion. Gerry's life had been cruelly taken away, and that person had to pay for it.

But would the police quit focusing on Phil and look for the real killer?

CHAPTER · 2

SUNDAY AFTERNOON, CAL PICKED ME UP FOR A VISIT TO SPANISH Point, a historic park just south of Sarasota in Osprey. He wore khakis and a navy polo shirt. He's only a couple of inches taller than I am, which is five-foot-six, and he's robust but not fat. However, the gray eyes are his most distinctive feature.

It had taken a while, but I'd finally convinced him not to touch up his hair anymore, and the white at his temples looked distinguished against his full head of dark hair. Evidently there were no balding genes in his mother's family. He'd told me recently he was going to let it grow out—a radical move for him—and I noticed it was a little longer, curling slightly over the edge of his ears.

Cal had been a small-town newspaper editor and now did freelance writing. He was researching a sidebar on Spanish Point for a longer article on the history of the Sarasota area, and he needed to refresh his memory about the place. I had never been there.

He was in high spirits as we drove the short distance south on Tamiami Trail in his ten-year-old Ford. With the windows rolled down, the glorious autumn afternoon almost made the summer's unbearable heat and humidity fade from our memories.

My short gray hair is nearly impervious to being blown about, and I'm not all that hung up on my looks, anyway. Cal doesn't seem to mind being seen with a lady who's fast approaching her sixties and willing to flaunt it.

We pulled into the nearly full parking lot. The lovely wooded grounds were a welcome respite from the burgeoning growth along Route 41, both north and south of the site. We headed first to the packing house and then to Mary's Chapel, both reconstructed buildings from the days of the Webb family, early pioneers in the area who grew and shipped citrus to Key West, en route to northern markets.

Then we followed the path to the most intriguing feature of Spanish Point—the midden, a huge refuse heap created by prehistoric Indians. Dug into the center of the midden is a unique archaeological exhibition that shows, behind glass, remains from the Indian culture scattered throughout the enormous mound of discarded shells. We sat through the presentation twice while Cal took careful notes for his article.

We wandered through the colorful gardens built by Bertha Palmer, widow of Potter Palmer of the *Chicago Tribune*. She had bought up much of Sarasota County in the early 1900s and had planned on building her winter estate here, but she died before it could be constructed.

Cal and I spent more than an hour following the paths that took us through formal shrubbery, sunken gardens, and a jungle walk. There was even a small stone aqueduct that carried water to the far reaches of the area.

We were headed back to his car when Cal tripped over a tree root near the edge of the parking lot and went sprawling on the ground.

I was beside him in an instant. "Are you okay?"

He grimaced, sat up, and rubbed his ankle. "I twisted it. I don't think it's broken, but it's damn sore. Not sure I can walk on it."

"Let me have your keys. I'll go get the car and bring it over here."

I drove his Ford across the parking lot and onto the grassy area where he sat. By putting his arm around my shoulders and grabbing hold of the door handle, he managed to pull himself upright. Hopping on his good leg, he opened the door and dropped into the passenger seat.

As I drove up the Trail toward the hospital, I contemplated the eternal question: Why does it always seem that you get sick or hurt on a weekend, when your doctor's office is closed and you're forced to endure the zoo called the Emergency Room?

We got a wheelchair at the entrance to the ER and went in to face The Inquisitor: name, address, age, insurance card—especially the last. After Cal ran the gamut, we were dispatched to the waiting room, which was packed, just as expected. His injury was not life-threatening, so it would likely be an hour or two before he got any attention.

"Look, we're going to be sitting here for quite a while," he said. "Why don't you go on upstairs and visit your friend Phil?"

"You sure you don't mind?"

"Hey, I'm a big boy. Maybe I can even find a girlie magazine to read." He grinned.

"Lots of luck," I said, viewing copies of *Family Life* and *Reader's Digest* lying about. "I won't be gone long."

"Take your time. I might even catch a few winks."

I found him a *Field & Stream* that was only a month old and headed for Phil's room.

Arlene seemed surprised when I entered the room, rising to welcome me.

"I'm here with a friend who hurt his ankle," I explained. "Just thought I'd drop by to say hi. How's your dad?"

"Same. Always the same. Right now I'm waiting for them to discharge him to the Brightwood Nursing Home."

I whispered, "What about the problem?" I realized it was ludicrous to say it was a problem, but I didn't want to call it by name in front of Phil. "Heard anything more?"

She shook her head. Lowering her voice, she said, "Nothing. I don't know what to do about that. I've got to get back to my job in Pittsburgh pretty soon or I'll lose it. And this could drag on and on."

"Have you thought of trying to find a job down here?" I asked. "At least until this situation is resolved."

"That would simplify things so much. But the custody agreement for my daughter says I have to stay in Pennsylvania."

A nurse came through the door, first searching the sleeping face of Phil's roommate, then stepping over to our side of the room. She was on the plump side, an older woman, with gray curls framing a plain but sweet face.

"Oh, there's Phil," she said and turned to Arlene. "Are you his daughter?"

"Yes, I am. Are you new on the floor?"

"No, no." The nurse picked up Arlene's hand and patted it. "I'm Clara McCarthy. I work on the oncology floor, where your mother was a patient of mine. Phil was there almost around the clock, so I got to know him well, too. I just heard about his stroke and wanted to come see him. I'm so sorry about both of them."

Arlene hugged Clara and said, "Before his stroke, my dad spoke of you. It's sweet of you to come."

"My mother has Alzheimer's, so I have some sense of what you're going through. I try to visit her at the home every day after work. It's so sad when they can't communicate."

The two women embraced again.

"Look, Dad's awake," Arlene said. She walked closer to the head of the bed and smiled down at her father. "Clara came to see you."

He tried to smile, but the effects of the stroke turned it, instead, into a grimace.

Clara went around to the other side of the bed and patted Phil's shoulder. "I just wanted to say hello."

He nodded slightly, looking pleadingly at her as though he wanted desperately to carry on a conversation. He did seem able to understand what was said to him.

She turned back to Arlene and gave a small, sad shake of her head. Arlene said, "Clara, this is Emma Daniels, from Dad's condo."

"Hello, Emma, so nice to meet you." She turned to Arlene. "I'm afraid I can't stay. We're shorthanded on my floor, so I took just a minute to pop in to see your father."

"I've made arrangements for Dad to go to Brightwood. They'll probably take him later today."

"I hope he makes a good recovery. It's possible, you know."

I could detect a shade of uncertainty in her voice. But she was trying, as we all were, to give Arlene some hope for the future.

After Clara left, it occurred to me that she might be able to give Phil an alibi. Or know of something that could clear him. I wondered if the police had talked to her.

"That's the way my mother affected people," Arlene said. "Everyone adored her." She sighed, apparently unaware of the people her mother had ticked off with her outspokenness. "Emma, I'm not sure Dad can see you back there in the corner. Why don't you come over here by me."

I walked over beside her and did my best to put on a positive face for him. "Hey there, Phil. You're looking good. Having Arlene here must be good medicine." My remarks seemed insipid to me, but what do you say to someone who can't answer you back?

He looked at me with what I thought was a smile, contorted as it was.

"I'm so sorry about your illness. Everyone's asking about you at the condo."

His mouth twitched a little, but his expression didn't change.

Suddenly, the immensity of this terrible tragedy nearly overwhelmed me. What just a week earlier had been an intact, loving family of three had been reduced to two survivors—one damaged and one desperate. And more than anything, I felt sorry for Arlene.

I tilted my head toward the door. "I need to get back to my friend. Could we talk a minute outside?"

She turned to her father and said, "I'll be right back, Dad," then followed me out into the hall.

"Look," I said, "I know you can't stay here for long, and you're going to be worrying about your father's situation as far as the police are concerned."

"I'm at my wit's end, I really am," she replied. "I must get back to my job and my daughter, and I've little confidence that they're going to keep me up-to-date on their investigation."

"I know a detective in CID." I'd met him when Cal had done a story on a special program at the Sarasota Police Department. Cal had taken him out to lunch for an interview and invited me along. "Perhaps he'd be willing to talk to me occasionally, and I could relay the information to you. I can't promise anything. But you might want to get in touch with Detective Caronis and tell him you'd like for me to be a go-between. See what he says."

She grabbed both my hands. "Would you, Emma? I can't tell you how much I'd appreciate that."

"As I said, I'm not even sure he'll do it. But if the request comes from you, it might carry some weight. And I've thought of something that might help your dad."

"What's that?"

"It occurred to me that maybe some of the people who knew your mom through her volunteering could vouch for your dad. Surely a few of them must know him well."

She gave a hopeful smile. "I'm sure they do. Dad would often pitch in when they needed drivers or someone who could build things."

"Do you have a list of the groups she worked with? If things start to get serious, I could contact some of the other people involved."

"My mother was extremely well organized. She kept files on every one of them. To tell you the truth, I don't have much spare time, between staying here with Dad and trying to handle Mom's estate. Could I just give you all the files? That would save me from having to go through them."

"Good idea," I said. "I'll come and pick them up. When would be convenient?"

"How about tonight? I should be home about eight."

"I'll come see you then. I guess now I better get back downstairs."

"Thanks, Emma."

Cal was still reading the magazine when I returned to the Emergency Room. "How was your friend?" he asked.

"Neither Phil nor his daughter is in very good shape," I replied.

"Mr. Murray." A nurse called out his name. When Cal raised his hand to indicate he was there, she came and pushed his wheelchair back to a treatment room.

An hour later he reappeared, limping slowly, with a walking cast on his injured foot.

I got up to meet him in the middle of the room. "Is it broken?"

"No, I tore a ligament. Have to wear the cast four weeks. What a bummer." He limped toward the cashier and took care of his bill.

Once we were out the door, I asked him if he wanted to stay with me so I could take care of him.

As he hobbled slowly across the parking lot, he got a devilish look in his eye. "I suppose I'd have to sleep in the guest bedroom."

I gave him my boys-will-be-boys look. "Yes, Cal, this is a purely platonic offer."

"Well, in that case, I'll take a rain check," he said. "Besides, it's my left foot, and since I have an automatic transmission, I can drive. I'll be fine."

When Cal dropped me off at home, I went out and sat on my balcony. The view across the Gulf was exquisite, shades of blue-green paling from horizon to shore, where calm waves broke in fringes of lacy foam. It was hard to realize on such a day that tragedies were still happening as had befallen Geraldine and Phil and Arlene.

A little after eight that evening, I took the elevator down to the ninth floor and the Stapleton condo. Arlene answered my knock and invited me in. I stepped into the foyer and followed her into the living room.

Most of the places I've seen on Siesta Key are decorated in one of two ways: full of somber antiques and a lifetime accumulation of knickknacks moved from their northern home, or brand new rattan or bamboo furniture, in shades of green and pink, that is de rigueur for a Florida home.

I'm guilty of the latter. Paul had urged me to sell our mishmash of family pieces and buy "Florida stuff" as he put it. I've regretted it ever since. Mine weren't fine antiques but a mix of family pieces and things I'd picked up on sale. They had a history, and I miss them.

The Stapleton home was sparsely furnished with twentieth century classics like a leather Eames chair, a sleek futon sofa in beige, a dhurrie carpet in shades of brown and green, and framed posters of photographs by Ansel Adams. The simple Craftsman-style tables held specimens from the beach as their only decor: A large starfish was displayed on an end table, and a simple basket on the coffee table was filled with perfect olives, cats' eyes, bright orange scallops, and curlicued worm shells. The total effect was serene.

It always amazed me that someone as flamboyant as Gerry would have such a tasteful home. She was an enigma—a puzzle I never completely understood. I wished I'd had many more years to figure her out, if that were possible. Not that it mattered. Her generous spirit was what counted.

Arlene bade me to sit on the sofa. She sat in the Eames and said, "Again, I can't thank you enough for your help. It's considerably more than I have a right to expect."

"Not at all, Arlene. Whatever I can do for you is piddling compared to what Gerry did for me. What's the situation with your dad?"

"Well, he was transferred to Brightwood late this afternoon. It seems like a pretty nice place, though it's hard to judge on first impressions."

"How do you think he'll adjust?"

"My dad has a way of taking most things in stride. Except Mom's death, of course. He'll never get over that, I'm afraid. I'm going to make sure he's settled in okay tomorrow and then return to Pittsburgh on Tuesday."

"Maybe I can drop in on him occasionally."

"You're very kind. I do hate being so far away from him, but he has many friends here, and he loves Florida so much. It would be cruel to take him back north."

And, I thought, *the police probably won't let him leave the area unless they can eliminate him as a suspect in Geraldine's murder.* Arlene, no doubt, was trying to put the best face on it.

"I need your address and phone number so we can keep in touch," I told her.

She got up and walked into the dining room and came back carrying a cardboard file box. "It's in the front of this. These are Mom's files."

We chatted a little longer, but I could tell she was exhausted, so I left. We hugged each other good-bye, and I could feel the faint trembling of her frail body. As I took the elevator back to my floor, I decided that Arlene was the saddest person I knew.

The next morning I went through the files, quite frankly more out of curiosity than anything else. I really wasn't at the point of needing to solicit character witnesses for Phil, since he hadn't been charged.

After all of the accolades that everyone had bestowed upon Gerry, I wanted to know more about her accomplishments. Though I knew she was involved in numerous community organizations, she seldom discussed her role in them. She was always far more interested in learning about the other person than in self-aggrandizement.

An amazing woman who apparently crammed forty-eight hours of living into twenty-four, she had served on the boards or was an officer in many organizations, including hospice, the Humane Society, a craft shop, Girl Scouts, and a pro-choice group. She kept meticulous notes on everything she did.

I took only a cursory glance through the vast majority of files because there was so much material and it looked pretty dull. The file for the pro-choice organization really aroused my interest, though. She'd been president nearly two years before, prior to my arrival in Sarasota. It looked as though she'd been rather high-profile at the time, given the news clippings I found. I couldn't help but wonder if she decided to opt for anonymity after some heated and highly publicized confrontations with pro-lifers.

One of the clippings included a photograph showing Gerry confronting a picketer in front of an abortion clinic. According to the article, she'd threatened to "sue their asses off" if they kept clients from entering the building. I'll admit I wasn't surprised that she would express herself in such an inelegant manner, and I admired her gumption.

Apparently she actually was the instigator of a suit filed against a small storefront congregation, whose pastor had advocated closing down the clinic by force if necessary. I had no idea what the status of that lawsuit was. No recent information on it was in the file. I wondered if it was ever resolved or if it came to trial.

I called Arlene and managed to catch her on the way out the door. I asked if she needed a ride to the airport the next day, but she said she'd be going directly from the nursing home and would call a cab.

"I have a quick question. Do you know anything about the suit filed against One True Light Church by the abortion clinic? It happened when your mom was president of the pro-choice group."

"Dad said something. Mom didn't want to worry me, but he thought I should know."

"Do you know if it was resolved?"

"I honestly don't know. Mom found out Dad was telling me about it and made him promise not to discuss it. She thought I had enough problems of my own. But I found out from their neighbor Mickey that she'd gotten some anonymous threats."

My heart did a little leap. "No kidding! What kind of threats? How did she get them?"

"Phone calls, I think. Maybe a letter or two."

"You didn't ask your mom about them."

"I couldn't. She'd been so adamant that I be kept out of it. I didn't want to get Mickey in trouble. But, of course, it worried me to death."

I hadn't seen any threatening notes in the file box, and I wondered if Gerry had kept them. Probably not, I decided. I doubt she even showed them to Phil, destroying them immediately. She had confided in her neighbor, though, presumably because she felt the need to share it with someone.

"Well, that happened so long ago, it probably isn't important. I'd just forget about it." I said that for Arlene's sake. I had no intention of forgetting about it myself.

CHAPTER · 3

I CALLED CAL. I WANTED TO KNOW HOW HE WAS, BUT EVEN MORE I needed his help.

"How's the ankle?" I asked.

"It's not too bad, but the cast is a pain in the butt. It makes it really hard to sleep."

"Poor baby."

"So what's happening with you?" he asked.

"I was wondering if you could do a little research on the Net for me."

"When are you going to get yourself a computer, Emma?" he asked for the umpteenth time.

"What am I going to do with it besides play solitaire?"

"Do your own research. E-mail Mark and your friends."

I couldn't see spending hundreds of dollars to do what little research I was interested in. And I could always use the phone. "I only ask you once in a blue moon to look up anything for me." I hoped I didn't sound whiny.

"I get it. This is why you quit your job at the insurance company some years ago, isn't it?"

"What are you talking about?"

"You're scared of computers," he declared. "I just realized it. I'll bet you quit because your office was on the verge of going high tech."

"Not true." Though he'd hit close to home.

Not long after I met Cal, I told him I'd resigned from my job in Columbus because Paul, who had accumulated far more vacation time than I had, wanted me to be available to travel with him whenever he could get away. I'd been greatly relieved because I knew that the office would be computerized soon. Although Paul had urged me to take computer courses, I always found an excuse. I'm still afraid I would prove to be a dummy.

"Okay, okay," he said grudgingly. "Stay in the Dark Ages. What do you want?"

I told him about the newspaper articles I found in the file and the supposed threats. "I was wondering if the paper had any other articles about One True Light or about the suit that Gerry apparently filed against them. Can't you access the newspaper's archives on the Web site?"

"It's going to cost you."

"I'll pay whatever expenses there are."

"It's going to cost you dinner tonight."

"You mean I have to cook?"

"Damn straight."

I sighed. I really don't like to cook. But it was worth the price. "Okay. Six o'clock."

"I'll be there with cast on."

Cal came limping to my door promptly at six. Punctuality is his middle name. I'd fixed spaghetti, which is not only a snap—especially if the sauce comes from a jar—but is one of his favorite meals. A tossed salad and garlic bread were all I needed to go with it. A fairly effortless payment for any information he might have.

I decided not to pester him for the results until after dinner. Given my overwhelming curiosity, I found it difficult to be gracious. It seemed to me he made endless small talk to needle me.

Finally we finished our dishes of chocolate ice cream, and I cleared the table. We went into the living room, where Cal sat on the couch and propped his leg on my glass-and-wrought-iron coffee table.

"So?" I said.

He grinned. "It's driving you nuts, isn't it?"

I leaned over and hit him playfully on the arm. "You're mean, you know it?"

He put his arm around my shoulder and pulled me to him. "I'm just wondering why you're so curious about all this."

"Oh, I don't know," I said blithely. "Since there was nothing in Gerry's files that gave a clue as to the outcome of the suit, I wanted to know how it all turned out. You know me, I gotta have the whole story."

Giving me a look that said "Don't kid a kidder," he withdrew his arm and searched in his pocket for a minute, bringing out some folded papers. "Okay. I'm giving this to you very reluctantly. Make of it what you will."

He had printed out several articles, two brief ones on the One True Light Church, and a couple about the suit.

The first one came from the religion page of the *Herald-Tribune*, which features a different church each Saturday. One True Light was formed in 1994 in a storefront on Central Avenue, and the Reverend Tom Guy Packard claimed its primary mission is to "stamp out the holocaust known as abortion," but the congregation also serves the needy and those "overlooked by our acquisitive Capitalist society."

Are these people liberal or conservative? I wondered.

The second article quoted an ex-member of the church as claiming that One True Light was actually a cult and that when the member dropped out, he was threatened by Packard. This was reported to the police, who investigated the allegation, but Packard denied it. Since there was no corroboration, the charges were dropped. That made me sit up and take notice.

Cal had been watching me.

"What do you think?" I asked him.

"About what?"

"About this man Packard. Does it sound to you like he's capable of murder?"

"Whoa, there. Aren't you overreacting? It sounds like he likes to mouth off. But whether it's just bluster or he's capable of homicide, I couldn't possibly say. There's not enough to go on."

The other articles were about the lawsuit. Evidently it had been settled out of court. So there was no way of knowing whether any major money was involved. I doubted if One True Light had much money to spare. If they'd been forced to pay the clinic a big sum, a whole lot of resentment could result.

"Thanks for doing this," I told Cal.

"Please tell me you won't go off and do something stupid."

"Me? Stupid? Never!"

On Tuesday mornings I deliver Mobile Meals, a service for older adults who are unable to cook. I usually work with another woman; one of us drives, while the other delivers the meals to the door. We are assigned to one of the poorest neighborhoods in Sarasota, which has made us thankful for our own good fortune.

I'm appalled at some of the conditions in which people live: rickety houses with tumble-down porches and steps, broken plumbing, no air-conditioning in the torrid summers, and inadequate or no heat on cold days. It's enough to make you cry. Yet, almost without exception, the people who receive the meals do not seem bitter and are extremely grateful for the food. It's a humbling experience.

My Mobile Meals partner had just left to tour Europe, and I decided I could manage alone for three weeks. I picked up the meals—twenty-four foam cartons containing meat and vegetables, milk and juice, plus dinner rolls and pieces of fruit—at a Methodist church parking lot near Tamiami Trail. I noticed that we had a new client as I read over the list that included instructions on how to reach each house or apartment.

The new client, number four on the list, was Rose Willis, and her house was the worst I'd visited. The porch looked so precarious, I was afraid it would fall on me or I'd go through the floor. The roof was in terrible shape; it had to be leaking. And the siding hadn't seen paint in many, many years.

The instructions said that Rose was in a wheelchair and I should let myself in. It took a few minutes for my eyes to become accustomed to the gloom. When I could finally see, I was appalled. Rose, a wizened, hunched-over lady, sat in her wheelchair in a corner of the room. Stacked everywhere were discarded papers, clothes, even dried-up food. The stench of mildew was strong, mixed with other unpleasant and unnameable odors. What little furniture she had was broken-down and dirty. Rose obviously had no one to help her.

"Hello," she said in a little bird-like voice.

"Hello," I replied. "I'm Emma Daniels and I've brought your meal. Would you like it on the table?" A beat-up table stacked high with papers stood beneath the filthy front window.

"Yes, please. That would be nice." She slowly rolled her wheelchair over to the table and pushed aside some papers, making a stack fall on the floor. She seemed not to notice. "Right here." She indicated the small cleaned-off spot.

"What about silverware?" I asked. "Do you have any?"

She pulled a spoon and fork out of her pocket and held them up to show me.

"Anything else I can do for you?"

"No, sweetheart. I just appreciate this so much. It's the first hot meal I've had in weeks."

"I'll see you next week then." I fled the house, the tears welling up in my eyes so much that I almost missed the step off the porch. *Why do people have to live like this?* I knew I had to get help for her.

I kept thinking about Rose as I delivered the other meals. The circumstances of the people on the rest of the list didn't seem quite so dire by comparison.

On the way back to the church to return the cooler, I had an idea. I'd been trying to think of a way to find out more about Tom Guy Packard, the founder of One True Light Church. In fact, I wanted to meet him, size him up. See if I thought he could in any way have been involved in Gerry's death. But I didn't know how to approach him. I didn't think he'd believe me if I told him I wanted to join his church. I'm not *that* good an actress.

What if, I wondered, I told him I found a woman who needs help and hoped he could get his congregation involved? After all, his was the closest church to her, just two or three blocks away. I'd tell him I'd like to work with them when they clean up her house. And just maybe I could get an earful while I was doing it.

After I returned home, I grabbed a bologna, cheese, and mayonnaise sandwich before driving to the police station on Ringling Boulevard. Arlene had called me just before she'd left that morning to tell me she'd talked with Caronis and arranged for me to see him at two o'clock.

The uniformed woman behind the counter in the lobby buzzed me through the door when I told her I had an appointment. I took the elevator to the third floor and walked down the corridor to the Criminal Investigation Division.

The CID secretary, a plain-looking woman with a severe hairdo, reminded me of my fourth-grade teacher, who had terrorized me.

"I'm here to see Detective Caronis," I told her. "My name is Emma Daniels."

"I'll let him know you're here," she said in a clipped manner.

While I waited, she glanced at me now and then with a scowl on her face till I was sure she instinctively knew all my fourth-grade transgressions. I was relieved when the detective came out to greet me. I was afraid the secretary was going to have me standing in the corner at any minute.

"Mrs. Daniels, good to see you again." He extended his hand.

I liked the firm, confident handshake that he gave. His hair, cut a little shorter than before, was more becoming to his squarish face, and he'd grown a mustache that was a shade lighter than his dark blond hair. His benevolent expression hadn't changed at all.

"Come on back," he said, leading the way to his cubicle.

I noticed a picture of his family on his desk—three children, one an infant in his wife's arms. "What a lovely family. And a new baby," I said. "Boy or girl?"

"That's Robert Jr.," he said, beaming. No wonder. The older children were beautiful little girls.

"I understand Arlene Caviness talked to you about the possibility that I could be a go-between for her and the police department. I know that since she's living in Pittsburgh, she's worried that she won't know what's going on."

Caronis opened his drawer and pulled out a pack of chewing gum and offered a stick to me.

"No, thanks."

"I'm trying to stop smoking," he explained, pulling out a piece, unwrapping it, doubling it over, and putting it in his mouth. "The school has taught my girls how bad it is, and they're all over my case." He smiled slightly, as if proud of his daughters for their chutzpah, and said, "The Stapleton case is at a standstill right now. Not much to tell you. If anything changes, I can let you know."

"Is that because of Phil's condition?"

He nodded. "He's not in any shape to question."

"What about other suspects?"

"It looks like a pretty straight-forward case of mercy killing. We haven't been able to come up with any other scenario."

"Did you know that Geraldine, as head of a pro-choice group, had worked with the abortion clinic to sue One True Light Church?"

"Right. We know about that. Mrs. Stapleton had reported she'd received threats. She showed us one letter she got and described the phone calls. We looked into it but concluded they were probably intended only to frighten and intimidate her, although we kept a pretty close eye on the situation at the time. The suit was settled out of court, and it's been almost two years since the threats. If they meant to carry them out, they'd have done it sooner rather than later. And they'd probably have done it in a much more dramatic way to provide an 'object lesson' to anyone else who dared support abortions. It was a fluke that we even found out she was murdered."

"I met a nurse from the oncology floor who had taken care of Geraldine. Clara McCarthy. I thought maybe she could give Phil an alibi."

Caronis opened a file on his desk and read it quickly. "Looks like she was interviewed. She was at the other end of the corridor when Mrs. Stapleton died. Couldn't say for sure whether Mr. Stapleton was with her or not. He did stay beside her almost around the clock, she said, but he could have gone for a bite to eat or something."

Oh damn, I thought. *There goes that bright idea.*

Things were not looking good for Phil. I didn't know whether to pray for his recovery or not. Life in a nursing home, as bad as it is, would surely be better than life in prison. But poor Arlene would have to retire in poverty after her father's assets were all used up.

C H A P T E R · 4

FROM THE POLICE DEPARTMENT, IT WASN'T FAR TO THE ONE TRUE Light Church, sandwiched between a used furniture store and an appliance shop on the fringes of downtown. Framing the door, two plate-glass windows, which once featured hardware or auto parts, were now covered with colorful crayon drawings by kids: spirited renditions of rainbows and birds, as well as houses with mommies and daddies and children. I'd expected to be put off by the place, but I found the display rather touching. ONE TRUE LIGHT was painted in black and gold Victorian-style lettering on each window, and a welcome sign graced the door.

I couldn't see inside, but I tried the door. As I opened it, a little bell tinkled, probably a holdover from the days as retail space.

The room, lighted by four white glass lamps hanging from chains, had been stripped of its counters, and I could see the imprints where they'd sat, leaving pale islands on the sun-darkened hardwood floors. Rows of inexpensive folding chairs faced an old oak podium that leaned slightly to the right. On the wall above it hung a rough-hewn wooden cross, lit by the one modern accessory in the room, a small spotlight. The rest of the white walls were lined with pictures of Jesus in many different settings, but always surrounded by children.

A door opened in the back, and a man emerged, pushing a tank of oxygen before him. The plastic tubing that connected him to it was tucked over his ears and under his nose. Painfully thin, he'd slicked back what was left of his graying hair so that it clung to his scalp like a skullcap.

"May I help you?" he asked, his voice breathy from what I assumed was emphysema.

"I'm looking for Reverend Packard."

"I'm Reverend Packard," he said.

How could this man have killed Gerry? I thought. No one could help but notice him tethered to the oxygen tank wherever he went. But then I realized that it didn't rule out the possibility he was *behind* her death.

"I wondered if I could talk with you for a minute."

"Of course," he said, indicating a chair in the front row.

As we sat down, Tom Guy Packard set the tank beside him like a pet dog. *What a way to have to live*, I thought.

"What can I do for you?" he asked.

"I'm Emma Daniels. I deliver Mobile Meals on Tuesdays, and this morning I had a new client who's in a wheelchair. The conditions she's living in are terrible. She desperately needs help, and I thought perhaps your congregation might be able to do something for her."

He looked at me thoughtfully. "Why did you choose One True Light for this?"

Don't tell me he sees through me already! "Because you're the closest church to her."

"Tell me, Mrs. Daniels—I'm assuming it's Mrs.—do you not attend a church?"

At least I didn't have to lie. "No, I don't. I haven't gone since I moved to Sarasota over a year ago."

"Were you affiliated with a mainstream church?"

Where is he going with this? "Yes. I'm Presbyterian."

"Perhaps you've been feeling that the traditional church is not meeting your needs."

"Perhaps."

"You know that unaffiliated churches are the fastest growing segment of the Christian church, don't you? We're going back to our roots, to the fundamental precepts of our religion. Mainline churches have strayed too far from our basic beliefs." The man had a way about him. There was something soothing—almost hypnotic—about his voice. I could understood how he might sway susceptible people.

"Look, Reverend Packard. I didn't come here to discuss my religious beliefs. I came to get some help for Rose Willis."

He had been leaning ever closer to me in his earnestness, and now he sighed and slumped back against the chair. "I'm sorry. Sometimes I get carried away. I know I haven't got too much longer to live, and I'm trying to bring as many converts to my church as I can before I go."

"I'm really sorry," I said.

"What kind of help does Rose need?"

"Her home is filthy and falling down around her. She needs a bunch of people to clean it up and do what repairs they can. I'll be there too, of course, but it's more than one person can do alone."

He nodded. "Our main focus, as you might know, is to overturn Roe versus Wade and to prevent as many abortions as we can in the meantime. But we are concerned with those in need too. Let me see what I can do. May I call you tomorrow after I've gotten in touch with some of my deacons?"

"That would be wonderful." I gave him my phone number, thanked him, and left.

I didn't know what to make of Tom Guy Packard. For some reason, I'd expected a burly fellow, someone who looked like he could pick a fight with anyone. But in reality, he was more a figure to be pitied. Now I assumed that the threat came from his ability to stir up the congregation with inflammatory rhetoric. From the little that we talked, I could see where he could be persuasive.

About ten the next morning, I received a phone call.

"Mrs. Daniels, Reverend Packard here," he said. "I talked to some of my deacons, and we'd like to help your lady. How about Saturday morning at eight? We could get the most people together at that time. We have a contractor in our congregation who's offered to supply any materials needed for repairs. Will you tell her we're coming?"

"I certainly will. And thank you so much. I'll meet you there on Saturday."

During the drive to Rose's house, I began to wonder if I hadn't been a bit presumptuous in arranging this without even consulting her. I'd gotten so carried away with my plan (and perhaps my own importance) that I never once considered her feelings.

But fortunately, Rose was overwhelmed with gratitude.

"A lot of people are coming?" she asked in her chirpy voice. "To help me?"

"Yes, Rose," I said. "They'll be here early Saturday morning, and they're not only going to clean up in here, they'll fix your porch and your roof."

Tears started streaming down her cheeks. "God is so good to me," she sobbed.

I was taken aback by her reaction. *Here you are,* I thought, *sitting in a wheelchair in abject poverty, and you're thankful to God.* I took her crippled hands in mine. "You're quite a lady, Rose."

She didn't reply but gave me a teary smile instead.

When I was back in the car on the way home, I realized how I'd always thought of Sarasota as the playground for the well-off retired set. I never once thought about people like Rose.

I decided to buy her a nice robe and slippers, since I didn't know what size dress she wore. A robe can fit anyone. I wanted her to look nice when the church members came on Saturday. And so I stopped at the mall and purchased a blue terry-cloth robe and satin slippers for Rose . . . to meet the people who could be responsible for Geraldine Stapleton's death.

On Thursday, I visited Phil Stapleton to see how he was settling in at his new surroundings. I'd told Arlene that I would check on her father from time to time, and I guessed the first weeks would be the most difficult for him.

Brightwood Nursing Home, only a couple of years old, is on the far east side of the city, where rapid growth is taking place, so I usually try to avoid going to that part of town. Housing developments, shopping centers, and offices are popping up like Jack-in-the-boxes, so fast that the streets are overwhelmed with the increased traffic.

I parked in front of the attractive one-story building that featured a red-tile roof, creamy stucco walls, and a portico with Spanish-style arches at the entrance. The reception area inside was papered in cheery flowers. A silk rose arrangement sat on the desk where a grandmotherly woman typed on a computer. She gave me directions to Phil's room, down the right-hand hallway.

As I walked down the corridor, I glanced into the rooms. Each was furnished with well-worn chairs and antique dressers that had been culled, I supposed, from the patients' own homes. Photographs of loved ones and drawings by grandchildren hung on the walls, and trinkets that no doubt held special memories cluttered the tops of dressers.

Every effort had been made to make the place as pleasant as possible, but the result was a poignant reminder of how everything is reduced to the basic essentials at the end of life. The sight of listless patients slumped in wheelchairs, staring blankly ahead, frightened me. I couldn't help but wonder if I'd be like that one day.

I was afraid this visit might be an exercise in futility, but hoped Phil would be aware that I was there. His room was at the back of the nursing home, which was built in a square, with a patio in the center where patients could be taken outside without fear they would wander off. Someone had placed a bird feeder on a pole outside his window, and it was alive with goldfinches. Phil was sitting in a wheelchair, his back to the door, staring out the window at the birds.

I walked around his chair to face him. "Hello, Phil," I said. "It's Emma Daniels from La Hacienda. How are you feeling?"

"Unnnhhh," he said.

I was surprised that he could make any sound at all. I didn't know if it was an involuntary sound or if he was actually trying to communicate with me. So I sat in the striped wingback chair in the corner of the room and talked to him for a few minutes. It's hard to know what to say when you can't expect an answer, so I talked about myself, chatted on about the weather, any kind of small talk to fill the uncomfortable silence.

His eyes seemed to comprehend, but his left arm, the one that wasn't paralyzed, twitched with a nervous tic. Was he responding to me, or was it uncontrollable?

An aide came bustling into the room. Short and stout, with café au lait complexion and blue-black hair, she wore a big badge, featuring a yellow happy face, on her ample bosom. "How are you today, Mr. Stapleton?" she asked cheerily, as if she had every expectation of an answer. "How nice you got company." She winked at me. "And will you look at those birds out there. They're having a reg'lar convention. I think they come just to say 'hey' to you." She patted him affectionately on the shoulder. "I'll come back after your company's gone to give you a bath."

I got up, relieved to have an interruption. I was running out of things to say. "I've got to go now, anyway."

"Don't rush off," she said.

"No, really, I do have to go." *What a cop-out,* I thought. *As if I have a million things to do.* "I'll come back soon, Phil."

The aide walked out into the hall with me. "Are you Mrs. Daniels?" she asked when we were out of Phil's hearing.

I stopped. "Yes, I am. Why?"

"When Mrs. Caviness brought her father in last Sunday, she told us about his 'problem.' You know what I mean? About her mom's death. And the police."

"She did?"

"Yes, she said we should know about it in case the police ever came to see her father."

"Then you know they suspect he's guilty of a mercy killing."

"Right. She told us that. And that she didn't believe it for a minute. She asked us to keep a close eye on him in case somebody tried to hurt him, too."

"Good." I was relieved she'd thought to do that.

"And she asked us to contact you if anything at all happened that seemed strange or out of line."

"Are you saying something did?"

She lowered her voice. "Yes. I was tryin' to make up my mind whether to call you. It might not be anything."

A shiver of dread coursed through me. "What happened?"

"When I went in his room this morning, I found a pillow over his face. He'd had a bad night. The night staff had given him strong pain medicine, and he was pretty out of it, so I think that's why he hadn't batted it away. But that means he probably couldn't have put it there himself. I wondered if someone had tried to smother him but had been scared away. It could've been one of our other patients. Even though we screen them so we don't bring dangerous ones here, sometimes their minds are so far gone, you never know what they might do."

"Did you report it to the person in charge?"

"I did. She thought it probably was an accident but asked us all to keep an eye on him. We're short-staffed, so we can't have someone with him every minute."

"I really appreciate your telling me. You say you have my phone number, in case something like this happens again?"

"Yes, ma'am. I certainly will call you. He's such a sweet old man, I'd hate to see anything bad happen to him."

Driving home, I ran our conversation over and over in my mind. Should I call Arlene? I decided it was too nebulous a thing to get her all worked up over. She had so much on her mind already, I didn't want to add to her burden unnecessarily. But there was one thing I did want to check out.

When I got home I called the hospital and asked for the oncology floor. When someone answered at the nurses station, I asked for Clara McCarthy. She was the only one I could think of who could answer my question about hospital policy.

"Hi, Clara," I said. "This is Emma Daniels, a friend of Phil Stapleton. I met you in his room the other day."

"Oh, yes. What can I do for you, Emma?"

"I just had a question about hospital policy. If a patient is transferred to a nursing home, would anyone give out that information over the phone? Or to anyone who comes in to see him, for that matter?"

"No. They would only say that the patient has been discharged."

"Okay, so it's not public information."

"No."

"Well, that's good. I was just curious. Thanks for your help."

"You're welcome."

Just as I started to hang up, I thought of something. "I remember he had a roommate at the hospital. If someone had called the room directly, couldn't the roommate have told them where he'd gone?"

"Oh, sure. That's entirely possible."

CHAPTER · 5

I WAS AT LOOSE ENDS AFTER MY CONVERSATION WITH CLARA. I debated calling Cal, but he was working hard to finish his article. He'd made his second bathroom into a darkroom, and he could very well have been holed up in there. So, though I would have loved to chat, I didn't want to interrupt him.

That evening, I decided to examine Geraldine's files more closely to see if I'd overlooked anything important the first time. I still wasn't letting Reverend Packard off the hook, however.

Again I marveled at Geraldine's involvement in so many projects. The woman was a paragon. It made me feel like a complete slacker. In addition to her volunteer work, she did crafts as well, creating mirror frames and wreaths from seashells, a popular art form in Florida. She'd never showed me any of her work—she was very modest about her accomplishments—but she'd belonged to a group that ran a crafts gallery on Main Street in downtown Sarasota. It was run as a collective, with the craftsmen taking turns in the shop, each one spending a day or two a month acting as salesperson.

In the gallery file, caught in the middle of a stapled sheaf of Xeroxed incorporation rules, was a used envelope that I hadn't seen before. On the back was a note that read, "Suggest an audit to Priscilla. There's something strange about the books." The envelope was postmarked September 10, not long before Geraldine's cancer diagnosis.

The file contained a list of gallery members, including Priscilla Renshaw. I planned to talk to her in the morning, since it was now too late to call. Anyone as involved as Geraldine was bound to cross paths with others who considered her either a gadfly or someone outright dangerous to their agenda. So maybe I was on the wrong track suspecting Reverend Packard and his church members.

Friday was overcast, with off and on showers. After almost two weeks of sunshine, I couldn't complain. And the lawns and flowers badly needed the rain. I waited till ten, in case she was a late sleeper, then called Priscilla.

"It's her day at the crafts gallery," a male voice responded when I asked for her.

I decided to take advantage of that serendipitous fact to visit the gallery, as I was very curious about it. Though I occasionally shopped downtown, I was more likely to go to Siesta Village or to the mall and stores on South Tamiami Trail.

I walked into Crafts From the Heart and found it larger than I expected, an indication that Sarasota was home to lots of busy crafts-men—all those retirees with time on their hands. Several customers browsed happily among the tables filled with ceramics, afghans, jewelry, wooden items, and much more.

I pretended to browse, too, until all the customers had left and the place was momentarily empty, except for the woman I presumed to be Priscilla. When she hadn't been waiting on someone, she sat behind the cash register, busily crocheting. I guessed she was in her seventies, a chubby little lady wearing sweats and running shoes, constantly pushing up her glasses that persisted in sliding down her nose. Her salt-and-pepper hair was worn down to her shoulders in a teenage style.

"Priscilla?" I said as I approached her.

"Yes." She smiled. "Can I help you?"

"My name is Emma Daniels, and I'd like to talk to you about Geraldine Stapleton."

Her smile vanished. "Poor Gerry. We're all just devastated."

"What I wanted to ask you was—"

Just then two ladies came in, talking animatedly. They approached Priscilla. "Do you have any pottery?" one asked.

Priscilla pointed to the rear of the shop. "Back in the corner."

After they walked away, I said, "I need to talk to you in private."

She looked a little surprised but didn't ask me why. "We close the shop at noon for lunch. Want to meet me at Dorrie's Lunchroom?"

We agreed to meet there, and I went to the library to pass the next hour. I hoped to catch one of the new bestsellers before they were all loaned out. No luck, as usual. I put my name on the waiting list and trekked empty-handed the three blocks back to Dorrie's, where Priscilla was waiting for me.

After we'd settled into the booth and ordered our food, she asked, "So, what about Geraldine?"

"She was an incredible lady, wasn't she?" I wanted Priscilla to be thinking good thoughts about Gerry, in hopes she'd be willing to talk to me.

"She was that. She was one of the founders of the shop, you know. She gave a lot of bored retirees a wonderful outlet for their skills. And a little extra spending money, too."

"Gerry had a knack for knowing what people needed," I added. "At least she did with me."

"How did you know her?" Priscilla asked.

"She was my neighbor on Siesta Key."

"La Hacienda, right?"

I nodded.

The waitress brought our burgers and Cokes, and we ate in silence for a while.

Finally Priscilla said, "So what can I do for you?"

"I have her files," I told her with no further explanation. She could think whatever she wanted about that. "And I found this note in the gallery file that said she was going to talk to you about possible irregularities in the books."

She nodded her head slowly up and down with a faraway look in her eyes, as if trying to decide what to tell me. Of course, she didn't have to tell me anything. She had no idea why I was questioning her. I could have been an undercover cop, an auditor, anything. She didn't ask. Maybe she was afraid to.

"I don't want to hurt the shop in any way," I said. "That isn't my intention at all."

Priscilla looked directly at me. "Gerry called me the week before she went into the hospital. She'd worked on Tuesday, and when no customers were there, she went over the books pretty carefully. Gerry had served as treasurer for a couple of organizations, so she knew what to look for. She said she didn't like the looks of things, that maybe we should have an outside auditor take a look."

I nodded, amazed that Priscilla was being so open with me, and made an "mmmm" sound to indicate I was very interested. Afraid of pushing it too far, I hoped she'd continue without my having to ask more questions.

She more than accommodated me. "I called a meeting of our board of directors to discuss it. That's a pretty fancy name for the three of us who kind of keep things running. Anyway, one didn't think we should spend the money to hire someone until we'd had a chance to look into it ourselves. And the other one was afraid that if word got out, the bad publicity might hurt our sales."

Priscilla's forthrightness emboldened me, and I said, "So nothing's been done?"

"We'd set up a meeting to go over the books together. It turned out to be the day of Gerry's funeral, so of course it was canceled. We haven't been able to reschedule it yet because Alice has been out of town."

"What do you think of Gerry's suspicions?"

Priscilla studied me for a minute as she finished off the remains of her cheeseburger. "I'm not sure," she said finally. "Sometimes I thought Gerry had become overly cynical and suspicious of people's motives. Maybe it was because she'd been active in so many groups and had found out that things often are not as they seem. There could be a simple explanation for whatever bothered her about the books. Or maybe someone *has* had her hand in the till."

"When do you think you'll know for sure?"

"Early next week. Alice is coming home Sunday, and we plan to get together on Monday." She studied me again. "Just why is it you want to know?"

I was beginning to wonder if she'd ever ask. "I represent her daughter, who lives in Pittsburgh. I'm trying to tie up loose ends for her." I held my breath, hoping that would satisfy her.

She stared at her glass of Coke, which she moved in slow circles on the Formica tabletop.

"Well, if she's concerned that her mother didn't get all the proceeds from her sales, tell her we'll be checking on it. But not to get her hopes up that it would amount to much money. We're pretty small potatoes, you know. None of us makes a living here."

That didn't surprise me. Crafts don't usually generate large profits. Most craftsmen earn about fifty cents an hour, if they're lucky. But if someone had been skimming off the top of everyone's sales, it could amount to a tidy sum from the sheer volume of work for sale. And if she was discovered, the penalty could be severe. It was enough to make me add another possibility to the list of suspects.

"I'm sure Arlene realizes that. I think she's looking for closure on everything her mother was connected with. She wants whatever her mother started to be carried through to completion. More in tribute to Gerry's desire to serve the community than for any expectation of financial gain for herself."

Wow! I impressed even myself with that little speech. Even if it was mostly bullshit.

And Priscilla swallowed it. "I understand completely. Tell her I'll report back to you on the outcome of our audit."

I felt pretty smug as I drove home. I could blow smoke with the best of them. And all for a worthy cause.

My answering machine had a message from Cal when I got home, so I called him.

"Sorry I've been incommunicado this week," he said, "but I finally got that article done."

"That's great. How's the ankle?"

"Doin' pretty well. Be glad when the cast is off, though. What's happening with you?"

I hesitated before telling him, because he tended to worry about me. But I knew it would all come out sooner or later, so I filled him in.

"You actually met Tom Guy Packard?" he said when I finished. "I thought you weren't going to do anything foolish." Though Cal seemed to be trying to keep an accusatory tone out of his voice, he didn't entirely succeed.

"I can't believe he's a threat, Cal. The man has to push a tank of oxygen around everywhere he goes."

"Do you think he'll be there tomorrow when you clean out that house?"

"Yes, to keep an eye on things. I don't think he could do any actual work."

"How about this idea, then: I could come along as your friend. Tell him I'm there to run any errands you might need. If nothing else, I can go get Big Macs for lunch. The two of us 'crips' can sit there and shoot the breeze. Maybe I could learn something."

That seemed like a reasonable idea. And I knew Cal would feel reassured about my safety if he was there too. As if there would be any threat to me while surrounded by people from the church. And as if he would be in any position to help me if there was.

At ten that evening I heard a distinctive, rhythmic rap at my door, my son Mark's way of letting me know he is knocking. I had no inkling he was coming to Sarasota. I rushed to open it and found him leaning against the doorframe, a grin on his face.

"My gosh," I said, giving him a big hug, "what on earth are you doing here?"

He picked up his duffel and followed me into the living room. "Hope you don't mind, Mom. It was a spur-of-the-moment decision."

"You're on vacation?"

"Sort of. I took some time off to job hunt."

"You're kidding. You mean down here?"

"I need to get out of Toledo. Too many bad memories there."

Mark had a very bad time in the spring when his wife left him for another man. On top of that, he lost his job because his company was downsized. His ego took a real beating. I thought things had been looking up lately, though. He'd been working as a computer consultant, and while making less money than before, he had only himself to support now. They were childless, and Cindy didn't ask for alimony. She always did make more money than he did, which was another sore point. He had probably just put on a brave front for my benefit.

It really was good to see him. He seemed more rested than he did the last time he came, just after his wife left him. He'd looked unkempt then, as if nothing mattered to him anymore. Now he was clean-shaven, with his dark hair neatly trimmed, and his brown eyes had regained some of their sparkle.

We chatted about inconsequential things for a little while, but we both were tired and went to bed before eleven. Before retiring I told him about my plans to help clean up Rose's house the next morning.

"Maybe I can go along and help out," he offered. Ever since he'd been a Cub Scout, Mark always wanted to assist people.

"Great. We need all the help we can get. Cal's coming too."

When I'd first started seeing Cal, Mark had a problem with it. He was still struggling to accept his father's death; and the fact I was seeing another man, even though it was only a friendship, didn't sit well with him. But in the ensuing months, he'd become more relaxed about it.

"It will be good to see him," Mark said.

Now that was really making progress.

* * *

The next morning we were greeted by a return of the sun. I joined Mark in his favorite breakfast of three strips of bacon and two scrambled eggs, hash browns, toast with jam, juice, and coffee. Did I need wonder why he was getting a little bit of a potbelly? Or why I no longer had the nerve to stand on the scales?

Mark and I were in the car by seven-fifteen, since we were going to pick up Cal before we went to Rose Willis's house. I had done up the robe and slippers in bright gift wrap, and we wanted to get there before the One True Light members, so she could be dressed for them.

Mark and Cal waited in the car while I went inside. If I'd thought Rose was appreciative of the meal I'd taken her on Tuesday, she was like a child on Christmas morning when I handed her the box.

She tore at the paper as fast as her gnarled hands would allow, squealing in delight as she pulled out the contents. "Oh, they're so beautiful!" she cried. "I've never had anything so beautiful."

I helped her out of her shabby wrapper and into the terry robe, and placed the slippers on her feet. She seemed to sit up straighter, her shoulders square, her eyes shining with pride. She'd been transformed by the modest gift. She was like a queen, ready to reign over the proceedings. I was deeply touched and humbled by her metamorphosis.

I called Mark and Cal to come inside to meet Rose. I could see in their eyes the effort it took not to react to the awful surroundings. They were graciousness itself.

We heard some vehicles stop outside, so the three of us went out to greet the helpers.

A late-model Cadillac, a Nissan pickup, and a small Toyota had pulled up to the curb, apparently having come as a caravan from the church. A jumble of good used furniture was piled in the back of the truck. I could make out an upholstered chair, a floor lamp, and some small tables, along with a ladder.

Several people piled out of each vehicle, all dressed in blue jeans and T-shirts. As Tom Guy struggled out of the Cadillac's passenger seat with his oxygen tank, the driver opened the trunk and pulled out tool boxes, power saws, and heavy extension cords. Someone lifted cleaning equipment out of the Toyota's trunk. Altogether there were six men, including Tom Guy, and two women, one young and one middle-aged.

After making introductions all around at the curb, we went inside and introduced the church members to Rose. All the attention made her eyes dance and her hands flutter like butterflies.

"Rose," I said, "it's lovely out today. Why don't you sit on the porch while we work in here."

She smiled blissfully. "I hardly ever get to go outside."

Mark pushed her wheelchair out the door to the far side of the porch, where the floor was still solid. Cal and Tom Guy settled in, side by side in the driveway, on folding chairs someone had brought. Men began pulling up rotten boards on the right side of the porch, while others climbed up on the roof. The sounds of hammering and sawing made quite a racket. The women and two of the men stayed inside to clean. We all stood contemplating the rooms before starting, intimidated by the monumental mess.

"I brought lots of trash bags," Richard said, "but what we really need is a Dumpster."

"We'll just have to haul the bags to the city dump," replied Arnold.

Christie Anne and I decided to work in the kitchen. Very pretty, in a Rubenesque kind of way, she couldn't have been more than nineteen or twenty. Her hair was a natural white-blonde, and she had striking blue eyes that seemed the soul of innocence.

Almost immediately she began talking about her faith. As we scrubbed the sink and stove, cleaned out the cupboards, and washed the window, she spoke of the role that the church played in her life. Under ordinary circumstances, I would soon have tired of such talk. But this time I was very eager to hear about One True Light Church.

"Reverend Packard is so special," she said, "so inspirational. We all would follow him to hell and back."

"I gather that stamping out abortions is the main focus of your church."

"Yes, ma'am. There is a true holocaust out there. We have to do everything possible to keep those babies from dying."

"Tell me, Christie Anne, would that include killing people who run abortion clinics or anyone connected with them?"

She stopped what she was doing and looked at me with a shocked expression on her face. She hesitated before saying, "No, ma'am, I wouldn't think so."

"You just said you'd follow Reverend Packard to hell. Would you follow him to prison for your beliefs?"

"Why are you asking this?" She seemed very distressed now.

"I'm just trying to understand your point of view. I have trouble trying to comprehend your virulent opposition to abortion."

Christie Anne laid down her dish towel and began to cry softly, burying her face in her hands. I hadn't expected her reaction. At last she spoke. "My older sister had an abortion several years ago. At the time, she thought it was okay. But it has messed up her life. She has nightmares about it now, and she's very depressed. Sometimes I think she's suicidal. That's why I feel the way I do."

I went over and put my arm around her. "I'm sorry, Christie Anne. I didn't mean to upset you. I just think that everyone ought to be able to make up her own mind about it."

She wiped her eyes with her fists. "Sometimes when you're young, you don't realize how it can mess you up. I don't want what happened to my sister to happen to others."

She was so overwrought that I decided to drop the subject, hoping someone else could tell me more about the church's policy on violence toward pro-choice supporters.

By noon we had made a pretty good dent in the dirt and rubbish. The piles of paper and trash had been bagged and loaded in the pickup for disposal. The windows had been washed and the floors swept, and the kitchen was spic-and-span. I hoped it would stay clean. The good used furniture brightened up the living room. The porch had been fixed, and the roof repair was well under way.

The men decided that they could paint the outside of the house in the afternoon; the sheer number of them would make quick work of it. Several church members went in the Cadillac to buy paint, and Cal drove to McDonald's to buy lunch for everyone.

The rest of us sat about on the patchy lawn taking a break. The older woman, Rachel, had walked around to the backyard, so I followed her. She was leaning against the trunk of a dead apple tree, smoking a cigarette. Deep worry lines made a furrow between her brows, and her worn look suggested that she'd led a hard life. Her whole demeanor was one of resignation: *Go ahead, Life, give me your worst shot; I can take it.*

"That reminds me of the tree I used to climb when I was a kid," I said, gesturing toward the gnarled trunk. "Fell out of it when I was seven and broke my arm."

She just nodded curtly and kept on smoking. She wasn't making it easy to start a conversation.

"Does your church do this kind of thing often?" I asked.

She shook her head and took another puff. Just as I was about to give up on her, she said, "We devote our energies toward ending Roe versus Wade. It's a plague on this earth." She sounded more educated than her appearance led me to believe.

"Oh, right," I said, as if it had just occurred to me. "Don't I remember that you picketed the abortion clinic a couple years ago?"

"We did. And we'd still be doing it if Reverend Packard hadn't put a stop to it."

"Why did he do that?"

"Because we got sued. And it cost the church a bundle. He said we could fight it in other ways. Less public ways."

"Oh," I said. "And how do you do that?"

She took one last puff and flicked her cigarette away, letting it fall into the straggly grass, where it glowed for a minute before dying out. "I'd rather not say."

And she walked away.

C H A P T E R · 6

AFTER WE WERE THROUGH INSIDE ROSE'S HOUSE, EVERYONE BECAME involved in painting the outside. Even Cal did what he could, painting for a while, then sitting down to rest when his leg bothered him. Mark really got into the spirit, painting with such abandon, he was covered with white daubs all over his face and hands. My son the clown. Christie Anne tackled the entire porch by herself after we wheeled Rose back inside.

It was an exhausting but very satisfying day; we didn't finish until seven o'clock. We left Rose all aglow in her newly refurbished home, singing her praises of One True Light Church. And I certainly had to give them credit for their hard work. Cal, Mark, and I could never have done it on our own.

"What do you want to do about supper?" Cal asked as we drove toward Siesta Key.

"I don't know about you guys," I replied, "but I'm exhausted. How about ordering pizza?"

"Sounds good to me," Cal said.

"Make it two," Mark added. "I could eat a horse."

After we got home, I was anxious to talk to Cal, out of Mark's hearing, but couldn't figure out how I was going to manage that. Fortunately, after the pizza arrived, Mark said, "If you two don't mind, I'm taking mine into the living room. There's a game I want to see."

I'd forgotten that Ohio State—Mark's and my alma mater—had a big game, one of the few played at night for the sake of television. But I decided I could sacrifice even that for the chance to talk to Cal privately.

We took our plates of pizza and our mugs of beer out onto the balcony. The Gulf sparkled with pinpoints of light as starlight danced on its rippling surface. The gulls called out to one another, and a soft breeze soothed our tired bodies.

"This is one of those times I wished I lived on the water," Cal said.

"Why don't you move over here? There's usually a place for sale."

"Three reasons. Probably couldn't afford it. I'd hate to give up my garden. And I figure some day a hurricane is going to take everything out along the beach."

"That's positive thinking."

He shrugged.

"So what did you think of Tom Guy Packard?" I asked.

"He's some tricky dude."

"What do you mean by that?"

"I think he's so fanatical in his thinking that he'd not let much get in the way of accomplishing his goals."

"Did he say anything you think is incriminating?"

"He's too smart for that," Cal replied. "He skirts the edge of it, but he knows just where to stop. For instance, he says God will smite all those murderers who kill babies. When I asked him if he considers himself an instrument of God's will, he would only say that he is insofar as he makes sure all his followers understand God's will so they can act upon their consciences. I couldn't pin him down any more than that. But it wouldn't surprise me that he could incite someone to commit murder in the name of God."

"I talked with the two women," I said. "The older one told me that since Gerry's suit, the reverend has told them they can fight abortion in 'less public ways' than picketing clinics. But she was very vague about it."

"I think these are dangerous people, Emma. I don't think you should be messing with them."

"Maybe so. There could be one or two members who've gone over the edge. But the younger woman had a sad story to tell and was in the church because of her sister's experience. She didn't seem like the type who would go beyond the bounds of decency. I'd be inclined to think that the majority are like her, sincerely believing they're doing the right thing to picket and protest but not harm anyone."

"It's the one or two nuts that I'm worried about. So many atrocious acts are committed in the name of religion. Whatever happened to Jesus' admonition to love one another?"

"Good question."

Mark stuck his head out the door. "We're tied with Penn State. You ought to come watch. It's a good game."

Cal and I joined him, cheering on the Buckeyes, who barely squeaked by. The final score was 24-21, and that was accomplished only in the final seconds of the game.

Mark offered to take Cal home, noting that I was about to fall asleep in my chair.

As Cal left, he whispered to me, "You be careful now."

On Sunday morning, Mark decided to walk down the beach. He invited me along, and I was delighted to accompany him. I usually try to walk to Point of Rocks, a half mile south, but it had been days since I'd taken my favorite stroll.

Crescent Beach was once named one of the ten most beautiful beaches in the world. Shaped like a new moon, its powdery white sand extends for a two-mile stretch in the center of Siesta Key's west coast. Siesta Beach, located near the village, can be crowded during tourist season, but the farther south you walk, the fewer people there are. Its southern point ends at a tableau of flat-topped rocks jutting out into the waves, where tide pools collect tiny creatures from the sea.

We walked leisurely along the edge of the Gulf, I, as always, on the lookout for special shells, while Mark splashed in ankle-deep water. The beach always brought out the kid in him. We were both silent for a while. Then Mark spoke, his voice serious.

"What do you know about One True Light Church, Mom?"

"Not a lot," I said innocently. I wasn't going to tell him about my ulterior motive for involving them the day before. He tended to worry about me far too much.

"Why did you ask them to help clean up Rose's house?"

"They were the closest church around." That was true. I just wasn't telling him the whole story. "Why do you ask?"

"I don't know. I got kind of a bad feeling about them."

"In what way?"

"I overheard a conversation I don't think I was supposed to hear."

I did my best to look shocked, but I was hoping he could tell me some really incriminating information. For sure, I hadn't gotten much. "Like what?"

"A couple of the guys—I think their names were Arnold and Bud, or something close to that—they were talking real low, and I don't think they knew I was painting right around the corner from them. They were talking about that 'damned abortion clinic' and how they were going to show them who had the upper hand next Wednesday. I never figured out how they were going to do that, but I didn't like the sound of it at all. I think you need to stay away from that bunch."

"Good gosh, Mark. You sure you didn't misunderstand them?"

"Oh, I don't think so. They may want to help out some poor soul like Rose, but I don't think all their intentions are benevolent."

"Well, not to worry. That was a one-shot deal. Rose is in good shape now, and I don't have any other projects for the church."

"Well, thank God for that."

Mark wanted to sunbathe for a while, and I told him I needed to go back home and do some housework. What I really wanted to do was call Detective Caronis when Mark wasn't around. Caronis had given Cal his home number when he was interviewed, and I'd weaseled it out of Cal. The detective answered the phone after many rings, sounding as if he'd just gotten up.

"Sorry if I woke you," I said after telling him who I was.

"That's okay. Had a late night last night, but I need to be up."

"My son and I were with a group from One True Light Church yesterday. He overheard a couple of the men talking about doing something at the abortion clinic on Wednesday. I thought you should know."

"I'll look into it. I have a source who can probably find out what's going down. But you and your son should stay clear of them. They're a bad bunch. At least, some of them."

"We will," I assured him, crossing my fingers. "They helped us fix up a woman's house. It was a one-time-only thing."

Although I'd found no clear-cut connection between them and Geraldine's death, I wanted to keep looking for one. Providing I could do it without making myself a target. Mark and Cal wouldn't appreciate that.

Mark was up early Monday morning, anxious to go to his interviews. I'd made a couple of casual comments Sunday afternoon that he might want to explore the job market in Tampa and Fort Myers, to make sure he didn't miss out on any outstanding opportunities. I received little response. But then, when I'd said it, he was half asleep on the beach.

I truly think it was the beach that had made him think of moving to Florida. He couldn't get enough of it. If I wanted to visit with him, I had to sit on the beach too, although I burn easily and usually restrict my hours there to early morning. Mark takes after his father. He never burns, just turns a beautiful golden tan. I keep warning him he'll look like a leather satchel by the time he's fifty.

Not long after Mark left, Caronis called. "I wanted to thank you for the lead on One True Light," he said. "We learned that they'd planned a butyric acid attack on the clinic for Wednesday."

"What's that?"

"It's a really nasty chemical. It causes severe nausea, and the victims sometimes have to be hospitalized. And it takes hazardous materials teams to clean it up. It's a mess."

"Did you arrest anyone?"

"Two of them. Arnold Shafner and Richard Thompson, better known as Bud. Of course, they've already made bail. I think the church raised the money."

"What about Tom Guy Packard?"

"We don't have enough to charge him with anything. He's pretty cagey. He eggs people on but doesn't get his own hands dirty."

I was beginning to feel a little nervous. "Do you think they have any idea who contacted you?"

"I don't think so. These guys don't know when to keep their mouths shut. It's not the first time they've gotten into trouble because they can't help but brag. But that doesn't mean you shouldn't be real careful."

Mark wouldn't be home till dinner time, and I just couldn't sit around twiddling my thumbs. So I drove downtown to Crafts From the Heart. Priscilla had said they'd be going over the books that day, and I wasn't convinced that she would let me know what they found. I decided I'd go under the pretext that I'd returned to buy something I'd seen the other day.

Priscilla and two other women were huddled over an account book at a small round table in a back corner. Someone else manned the cash register.

"Oh, hi." Priscilla looked up and recognized me as I approached them. "You didn't need to come down. I was going to call you."

"I kept thinking about something I saw in here on Friday. I was sorry I didn't buy it then, so I came back before someone else got it first."

"Oh, fine, Emma," she said and introduced me to Alice and Catherine, the other two members of the "board." Both appeared to be in their seventies, and while Alice was petite and dark-haired,

Catherine was buxom and bottle-blonde.

I shook their hands. "How's it going?" I asked, wondering if they'd be honest with me. They might not want an outsider to know if the books had been cooked.

Priscilla pulled out the fourth chair. "As long as you're here, we might as well tell you what we found."

I sat down between her and Catherine.

"See here," Catherine said, turning the book around so I could read it. "Some of these sales prices sure do 'pear to me like they're bogus. This one, for instance, number 10-52. We all got membership numbers, and mine is 10, and 52 was an afghan I crocheted. And a real pretty one, if I do say so myself. Well, I'm whatcha call a compulsive record keeper, and I have this li'l notebook with all my item numbers and their prices. Too bad I didn't check out the books sooner, 'cause it was s'posed to sell for $50, but it's marked in here as $35. You see, we can mark things down after sixty days to get the old stuff out of the store, but when I checked it out, it was marked down after seventeen days. Only, I don't think it really was. I think somebody wrote $35 down in the book, but really sold it for $50, and kept the difference."

"Who keeps the books?" I asked.

"Everybody," Catherine replied. "The day you work, you write all the sales down."

I looked around at them. "So you can tell by the date who entered those numbers?"

All three nodded solemnly.

"How much do you think has been taken, altogether?" I inquired.

"We figure it's in the thousands," Priscilla answered. "The person works two or three days a month, and this has been going on since the shop opened five years ago. We were all too trusting. And we're all a bunch of amateurs when it comes to bookkeeping." She looked absolutely disgusted at their discovery. "I can't believe it went on so long before anyone noticed. If it hadn't been for Gerry, it would still be going on. Our checks go out every three months, so unless you're paying close attention to the numbers, you accept it at face value. We're just so tickled to have a little extra income, we never thought to question it."

I knew this revelation came as a shock to all of them. "So now what happens?"

Catherine, deep in thought, ruffled the pages of the ledger. "We all considered this lady a real friend," she said. "We're just all shook up over this."

Alice spoke up for the first time. "We feel like we should talk to her, see if we can't straighten it out ourselves without going to the police."

"Right," Priscilla added. "We sure don't need the bad publicity. And we want to try to understand why she did it. Does she have a mental problem? Is she in desperate straits? We're not ready to throw her to the wolves just yet."

"We planned to go over there now," Catherine said. "Why don't you go with us, Emma? You can be representin' Gerry's daughter."

"Okay, I'll do that." I hadn't thought I'd get the chance to become personally involved to this extent, but my curiosity was aroused now, and I was very interested in seeing how the guilty person would react. Could she have known Gerry suspected she was embezzling, and therefore killed her?

The women got up and started to leave.

"Emma, why don't you ride with me," Priscilla offered. "I have to come back to the shop with the ledger, afterward. Oh, and don't forget the thing you came to buy."

I looked around in a panic, my eyes lighting on a ceramic spoon rest shaped like a scallop shell. "Here it is," I said. "Perfect for my kitchen." I paid the woman at the cash register and followed the others out of the shop.

Alice and Catherine rode together, and I got in Priscilla's 1989 Toyota that had faded to a sickly green.

"So, tell me about this person," I said as we headed east on Ringling Boulevard.

"Maria is originally from Cuba. She and her husband immigrated to Miami back in the '60s. When her husband died some years ago, she decided to get out of Miami because there was too much crime there. Kind of strange, isn't it?"

"Yeah. Pretty sad."

Priscilla made a jog onto Fruitville Road. "Tell me something," she said. "I have a friend who works at the newspaper. He heard some rumors that the police think Gerry's husband might have killed her. Does Arlene know this?"

So the word was leaking out. I felt like I was caught in the middle. But I decided that honesty might be the best policy here. I hoped I wasn't making a mistake.

"She has heard that. Frankly, that's why I'm involved. We can't believe there's any truth in it at all."

"The poor guy has no alibi?" Priscilla asked.

"You didn't know he had a stroke and can't speak?"

She was so startled, she steered into the other lane, heading toward an oncoming car. At the last second, she whipped it back into the right lane as I clutched the dashboard and steeled myself for disaster.

"Oh, no!" she managed to say. "That's awful."

I settled nervously back into the seat and tried to keep my voice steady. "Let's keep this between the two of us, okay?"

"Sure."

We turned right on Beneva and drove a number of blocks till we pulled into Live Oak Trace, where rows of one-floor units surrounded a central area that boasted one live oak tree beside a small fenced-in pool. I wondered whose bright idea that was as I watched its slender leaves flutter down upon the water, making it a nightmare to keep clean. A blue Ford sedan was parked in front of C-12, which Priscilla had pointed out as Maria's. We pulled up beside it, and Catherine and Alice parked in the next slot over.

"Okay," said Priscilla as we gathered in front of the condominium. "Let me do the talking. At least, at first."

A woman in her fifties answered our knock. She was about my height and a little on the heavy side, but she had lovely Hispanic features. She wore a T-shirt and shorts and flip-flops but was carefully made up.

She seemed very surprised to see us. "Priscilla! Hi! Catherine and Alice, what are you all doing here?" The accent was slight, having softened over the years. She looked at me intently, as if trying to recall whether or not she knew me, and ended up giving me a curt nod.

"May we come in?" Priscilla asked.

"Well, sure. You'll have to excuse the mess." She stood back and ushered us into the living room.

The small condo had a tiny corridor kitchen that opened into a living room lighted by high clerestory windows. It was furnished simply with old but highly polished tables and a couch covered with what might have been one of Catherine's afghans. The "mess" consisted of the morning paper strewn about an easy chair, as if she'd been interrupted while reading. Everything else was spotless.

"Sit down, sit down," Maria said.

"I'd like you to meet Emma Daniels," Priscilla said. "Emma, this is Maria Alvarado."

"So nice to meet you." Maria gripped my hand firmly.

"You, too," I said.

We all settled in, Priscilla and I on the couch, Catherine and Alice on chairs pulled out from the dining table, and Maria in her chair. "To what do I owe this pleasant surprise?" she asked, smiling at us.

I felt embarrassed and sorry for her. She seemed so pleased by our unexpected visit, and we were about to drop a bomb on her.

CHAPTER · 7

PRISCILLA HELD A THROW PILLOW FROM THE COUCH IN HER LAP, nervously running her fingers along the edges. "Maria," she started, her voice almost breaking, "this is very painful for all of us."

Maria's smile disappeared, and apprehension stole into her expression. "What are you talking about, Priscilla?"

Priscilla leaned down and reached into the carryall she'd brought with her. She pulled out the ledger and laid it, unopened, on top of the pillow on her lap.

Maria's eyes narrowed slightly, although I could tell she was trying very hard not to react. I wondered if she would attempt to stonewall us.

Priscilla said very evenly, "I think you know, Maria. We're talking about the account books from the shop."

Maria's forehead wrinkled in concern. "Didn't I add or subtract right? I'm not very good at math, you know, even when I use a calculator. I hope I didn't screw up."

Priscilla bit her lip, bracing herself for what she had to say. "You sure screwed up this time, Maria. Ever since you started. You listed sales at less than what you actually got, didn't you?"

"How can you say such a thing?" Maria sat upright, radiating self-righteousness.

"Because Catherine keeps careful track of what she's put in the store. She checked back through the books and found that many of the things were marked down way before the sixty days were up. But we think you actually sold them at the original price and pocketed the difference." Priscilla's hands were shaking slightly now, from nervousness or anger.

Catherine added, "I just never dreamed that my checks from the store weren't right. I guess I'm a fool to think everyone could be trusted."

"That extra money," Alice chimed in, "makes a big difference for all of us who are on fixed incomes. You, of all people, should understand that, Maria."

After several moments of tense silence, Maria turned to me and burst out angrily, "And who the hell are you?"

"I was a friend of Gerry Stapleton. I'm representing her daughter."

"And what's she got to do with it?"

"Gerry's the one who first noticed something was wrong with the books," I replied. "Now that she's gone, her daughter, Arlene, wants to see that whatever her mother started is carried out. A way of honoring her memory."

I choked a bit on that, but since I'd told Priscilla a similar story, I had to stick with it. Besides, I could hardly say that I was considering her a possible suspect in Gerry's death.

Another silence. Finally, Maria muttered under her breath, "Damn Gerry Stapleton." Then she burst into sobs.

No one moved at first. We all sat like dummies, not knowing whether to comfort or condemn her.

Then Priscilla got up and put aside the ledger, seating herself on the arm of Maria's chair. She began to stroke her hair. "Why, Maria, why? You know we all care about you. What made you do such a thing?"

At last, her sobbing subsided. She looked up at Priscilla, her makeup destroyed by her tears. "I'm so sorry, I'm so sorry. Please forgive me."

Catherine pulled her chair over next to Maria's. "Honey, we simply don't understand why you'd do somethin' like this."

Maria pulled a Kleenex out of her shorts pocket and wiped her eyes and blew her nose. "My mother lives in Havana. She's in her seventies now, and life there is very harsh. She needs help so badly. And I can barely make do for myself on my income. You know I work as a baby-sitter whenever I can, and I have a little pension from my late husband. At first, I thought I'd just borrow a little from the shop to send her, and I planned to pay it back. But things just kept getting worse for her, and I couldn't seem to stop." She shook her head and looked down at the floor in utter defeat.

"So that's where it's all gone?" asked Priscilla.

"Every penny."

"You know, Maria," said Alice, "if you'd told us about your mom, we could have all pitched in and sent her something every month. You didn't have to steal it."

Maria flinched, as if she'd been struck. "I never thought of it that way," she said in a tiny voice. "I always thought I was borrowing it."

Priscilla moved back to the couch. "So what are we going to do about this?" she asked of everyone in general.

Maria looked at her, the tears beginning to flow again. "You won't turn me in to the police, will you?"

Priscilla looked from Catherine to Alice. "What do you two think?"

"I don't know," Catherine said. "It don't seem right for her to get away scot-free."

Maria looked as if she wanted to crawl under her chair. The transformation from the person who'd met us at the door was complete.

"It's not like she was taking the money for herself," Alice countered. "Maybe what we ought to do is write a letter to everyone who's in the cooperative, ask them to come to a meeting, and take a vote. I personally think it wouldn't do anybody any good to prosecute her. It's quite obvious she isn't going to be able to pay it back. Would it serve a purpose to send her to jail?"

"I think your idea of a general meeting is good," Priscilla said. "It's only right to get everyone's input on it."

"I'll go along with that," Catherine agreed.

Priscilla stood up. "I'm sorry this had to happen, Maria. We'll have our meeting as soon as possible and get back to you on it. I hope we can work something out."

Maria nodded numbly.

"We'll let ourselves out now," Catherine said. "Good-bye, Maria."

Maria only stared at her lap as we left the house. None of us said anything as we got in our cars to return to the shop.

We were almost downtown before Priscilla spoke again. "I liked Maria so much. I just can't believe this happened."

I wondered why she used past tense when speaking of her feelings for her friend.

After we'd returned to the craft shop, I left the three of them composing a letter to announce the meeting, set for Saturday afternoon. Priscilla said I was welcome to attend if I wished. I told them I'd be there.

I drove home to fix some lunch. I took my turkey, cream cheese, and cucumber sandwich out on the balcony and watched two pelicans riding the updrafts created by our building, one of my favorite forms of entertainment.

Perhaps it was watching them dive into the water to catch fish that reminded me I had to do Mobile Meals the next day. I'd found it exhausting to make the rounds by myself. Having to drive, read instructions, put the meals together, and take them to the door took twice as long without a partner.

I wracked my brain for a helper. I knew I couldn't find anyone at La Hacienda because so many units sit empty between April and November, when their owners are at their alternative homes. Our building takes on the appearance of a ghost town for nearly half the year. Those who stay year-round are usually the physically frail who can no longer make the long trip back and forth.

I was the exception, in that I couldn't afford a second home to get away from the oppressive heat and humidity of Florida summers, as much as I would have liked to.

And then inspiration hit me. I would invite Christie Anne from One True Light Church to go with me. She'd shown concern and compassion for Rose, and I figured I could question her while we drove around.

She'd told me her last name was Griffin and that she lived on Browning Street and worked the four-to-midnight shift at a convenience store. I found a J. P. Griffin on Browning in the phone directory. I was sure Christie Anne wasn't married, but she could have been living with her parents, so I dialed the number.

I recognized her sweet little-girl voice immediately. It reminded me of Melanie Griffith.

"This is Emma Daniels," I said.

"Oh, yes, ma'am. You're the lady at Rose's house, aren't you?"

"I am. I wonder if you could help me out." I explained all about Mobile Meals and that my regular partner had gone out of town.

"Sure. I'd like to see Rose again. And it would be good to help those other people. What time?"

I arranged to pick her up at nine-thirty.

I spent the rest of the afternoon catching up on routine chores I'd neglected. I knew if I didn't do a washing soon, I'd have to join a nudist colony.

Mark came dragging in at six, looking worn out. I felt that I should let him recoup before bombarding him with questions. He watched the evening news while I prepared dinner.

I fixed hamburgers and macaroni and cheese—not exactly a feast, but one of his favorites since childhood. No gourmet meals are necessary to please him.

He still didn't have much to say after we sat down to eat.

Finally I couldn't stand it any longer. "Well, how did it go today?"

He held up his hand, palm down, and waggled it back and forth. "So-so." He wasn't smiling.

"What does that mean?"

"The pay's not too hot."

"Is that important to you?"

He looked at me like I'd asked the dumbest question in the world. "Of course it is."

"More so than any other consideration?" It really wasn't any of my business, but the younger generation seems to have a different take on this than my generation does. I really wanted to know how he felt about this issue. "What about job satisfaction? Quality of life? Whether or not you fit in with your coworkers?"

"That's all tied up with how much you earn, isn't it?"

I couldn't believe what I was hearing. It was obvious we were poles apart on the matter, and I decided not to pursue it any further. "So, what's next?"

"I have some more interviews here in town tomorrow. Then on Wednesday, I think I'll go to Tampa. They might pay more up there."

After we finished eating, Mark went for a walk on the beach while I opted to stay home to see a TV movie. He'd been gone about fifteen minutes when the phone rang.

A strange, muffled voice, so disguised I couldn't tell whether it was male or female, said in a malevolent hiss, "Butt out. You'll be damn sorry if you don't." The receiver then slammed in my ear.

I shuddered and hung up with a shaking hand. That was no crank call. Whoever called was deadly serious—I was sure of that. But who could it possibly be? Someone from One True Light Church? Maria Alvarado? Someone I didn't even know about yet but who knew I was snooping around? Was this the same kind of call Gerry had gotten?

I couldn't watch television after that. All I could do was sit and think about what to do next. Should I tell Mark? I didn't think so. I saw no point in getting him upset. He would just cancel all his appointments to sit home to hold my hand, and I'd feel like a prisoner in my own home.

Should I tell Caronis? I decided to call him in the morning, but the threat was so vague, I doubted the detective could do much. He certainly wasn't going to assign me security around the clock on the strength of one phone call.

I would just have to watch my own back and try not to take any risks. Besides, other than seeing Christie Anne the next day, I'd pretty much come to a dead end. Was she a threat? Surely not. She seemed so honest and aboveboard that there didn't appear to be a devious bone in her body. Not that I don't sometimes misjudge people.

The next morning Mark left early again, and I called Caronis and told him about the call I received the night before.

"I want you to be extra careful," he said. "I'm not real sure what's going on here, but it could be that Bud and Arnold, from One True Light, are trying to intimidate anyone who might have ratted them out about the attack on the clinic. I'm pretty sure they don't actually know who it was, but they're probably trying to cover all the bases. We'll keep a close eye on those guys for a while."

I wasn't totally relieved by our conversation, but I couldn't spend the rest of my life holed up in my home. And I felt sure that delivering Mobile Meals wasn't going to put me in jeopardy.

I drove over to Browning Street, and Christie Anne came bounding out of the small stucco ranch the moment I pulled up to the curb.

"Good morning," she said, climbing into the passenger seat. "I'm so glad you asked me to do this." She radiated good cheer and energy. Oh, to be nineteen again.

We picked up the meals at the church and began our rounds; I drove and Christie Anne delivered the food. As we went from home to home, I questioned her about the arrest of Arnold Shafner and Bud Thompson.

"Did you have any idea that they were planning an acid attack on the clinic?" I asked.

"No. I was so shocked. I don't believe you ever win people to your way of thinking with violence. They brought shame on One True Light."

"Don't you think Reverend Packard eggs them on to do that kind of thing?"

We'd stopped in front of a run-down apartment, and Christie Anne spoke with passion. "The reverend is against abortion, with all his heart. But I never thought he was telling us to hurt anybody. I always thought he meant we should speak out and demonstrate and work to show others God doesn't want us to kill babies." She looked down at her hands on her lap. "But maybe . . . maybe I was wrong about him." Her voice got softer. "I don't know anymore."

I patted her hands. "Christie Anne, I know you want to do the right thing. I understand your feelings about abortion, even though I don't agree with you. But, above all, we agree that hurting people doesn't accomplish anything. Right?"

She nodded without looking up.

"Let me ask you something. In light of what Arnold and Bud had planned to do, do you think anyone in the church would consider killing someone? I know I asked you that last Saturday, and you said 'no way.' Would you reconsider your answer now?"

She turned and looked at me, her eyes wide. After several seconds, she said, "Maybe I have to. I can't believe what's happening. How could I have been so stupid?"

"You're not stupid, Christie Anne. Just sincere about your beliefs, and unwilling to believe the worst about anyone."

"I'd better carry the food inside, or we're going to get way behind," she said, hopping out of the car as a way to end the conversation.

I knew I would have to tread carefully, for fear of getting her so upset that I'd get nothing more from her.

The next stop was Rose's house, and we both went in to see her. The house was spotless.

Rose was wearing her new robe and slippers. She'd combed her flyaway salt-and-pepper hair, which had been tangled and oily the first time I saw her. "How are you ladies today?" she greeted us with a smile.

We assured her we were fine.

"Ya know, one my neighbors saw all the commotion here Sat'day. She never come over here before. But now she says she'll come ev'ry Monday and sweep and dust for me. Ain't that nice?"

Doing something for others can be contagious. That was good news, indeed.

After we left Rose's, Christie Anne seemed very contemplative. Finally, she asked, "Why do you keep asking me about whether or not anyone from the church might kill someone?"

"Did you ever know Geraldine Stapleton?"

She thought a minute. "I don't think so."

"She used to be president of the pro-choice group."

"If it's longer ago than a year, I wouldn't know her. I've only been in the church since last Christmas. That was when I went to hear Reverend Packard preach and decided I wanted to help the cause."

"Well, Mrs. Stapleton sued your church over the fact that they'd blocked the entrance to the clinic and were trying to shut it down. It was settled out of court, but I understand One True Light had to pay quite a lot."

"Ohhhh," Christie Anne said, as if it had all suddenly become clear. "So that's why the reverend's always begging us to pledge more. There's a lot of talk about how bad off we are financially, but I never knew why."

"Mrs. Stapleton died a couple of weeks ago."

"What? How?" Christie Anne's face registered wariness; she knew she didn't want to hear what was coming next.

"She was smothered. While being treated for cancer in the hospital."

Christie Anne put her hands up to her mouth in a gesture of horror. "Are you saying. . . ?"

"I'm not *saying* anything. But I sure am suspicious."

She looked ill. "You don't mean. . . ." She seemed to deflate in front of my eyes.

"I'm not accusing anyone," I said. "I'm just trying to find out who could have wanted Mrs. Stapleton dead. It's true it's been a while since the suit was settled, but some people carry grudges for a long time. And when they see an opportunity to do something about it. . . ." I didn't think it necessary to finish the sentence.

Christie Anne was silent until after she'd delivered the food at the next house. She was obviously suffering anguish over whether to tell me anything. When she got back in the car, she said, "Someone from the church works at the hospital. She might have known that Mrs. Stapleton was a patient there."

"Who's that?"

"Rachel Greeson. She was with us at Rose's house last Saturday."

"Oh, right." I remembered talking to Rachel in the backyard. She'd told me they were working against abortion "in less public ways." Well, killing someone without claiming responsibility would certainly be less public.

"I can't believe she'd do anything like that," Christie Anne added quickly. "She's kind of a strange lady, but she seems nice enough. She even offered to teach me how to knit. I've seen some of the cool sweaters she's done."

Christie Anne prattled on, and I knew she was having a hard time accepting that anyone from her church could be party to such terrible crimes. "But, of course," she said, "Rachel could have told other people that lady was in the hospital."

"It might be just a coincidence that she works there," I said, "but since I found out what Bud and Arnold are capable of, it does seem possible that she might have told them about Geraldine being in the hospital. It could have been their first chance to retaliate for the lawsuit with little chance of being caught."

She stared at her hands on her lap for a minute, then said, "I guess I'm going to have to find me another church."

"I think that would be wise. You don't want to be tainted by what the other members do. No matter how innocent you are, you'll be deemed guilty by association."

We finished our deliveries, and I dropped her off at home. "Let's keep in touch," I told her.

She smiled. "I'd like to. Call me if you need me again for Mobile Meals."

I was becoming fond of Christie Anne. In spite of her naiveté, she was a fine young woman. Even though we disagreed on the issue of abortion, I admired her sincerity and generosity.

CHAPTER · 8

AFTER LUNCH AT A BAGEL STORE, I DID A LITTLE GROCERY SHOPPING. When I arrived home, I checked my mail, which is delivered to one of the locked boxes just off the lobby. The Christmas catalog season had already begun, and I'd received stacks of mail every day, most of it thick volumes that lured me like siren songs. I could spend hours looking at them. This day was no exception, and I took the pile up to my condo, my groceries stashed in a little wheeled carrier that I pulled.

After putting away the food, I went through the mail and came across a large manila envelope with no return address. It was rigid and somewhat lumpy, and I couldn't imagine what it could be. I do occasionally order gift items from the catalogs, though I didn't recall having done so recently.

But that wasn't so strange, since my memory isn't what it used to be. I call those lapses "senior moments."

I wondered with amusement if the reason for no return address was because someone had sent me pornographic material by mistake. And then I became not so amused. I'd watched a cop show earlier in the week where someone was killed by a letter bomb.

After the threatening phone call, I decided not to take a chance—even if I ended up looking foolish. I wasn't about to stay anywhere near the thing, so I went back down to the lobby and called 911 on the public phone.

"Best you wait downstairs," the dispatcher said after I explained why I was calling.

"Don't worry. I'm already there," I assured her before we hung up.

As I sat on one of the lobby's striped sofas, hugging myself to stop the shaking that began when the full impact of my situation hit me, I thought how glad I was that Mark was gone. Before long, a squad car pulled up outside the front door. That set off new tremors, and my legs felt wobbly as I hurried to meet the cops.

Two uniformed officers entered the building. I was surprised they weren't wearing special armored suits.

"I'm Mrs. Daniels, who called you," I said.

"I'm Officer Mizenhimer," said the tall, lean one with prominent ears. "Can you tell me why you think there might be a bomb?"

"I received a threatening phone call," I said. "It wasn't specific, just that I'd be sorry if I didn't butt out, or words to that effect. I'd given a report to Detective Caronis in CID about something I'd overheard involving the abortion clinic, and I think the guys that I implicated might suspect I got them arrested. I'm pretty sure I haven't ordered anything that would be sent through the mail, and the envelope just looked suspicious to me. Maybe I'm overreacting, I don't know."

"No, you did the right thing," the other officer said. "You don't want to take chances. Can you describe the envelope?"

I relayed as much detail as I could recall.

"We want you to stay here," he said when I'd finished. "We'll clear out the floors above and below you, as well as your own, and alert the fire department, EMS, and bomb squad. What's your condo number?"

"Eleven twenty-three," I said, giving him the key. "The package is on my kitchen counter."

I paced the floor for a while, too nervous to sit still as the cops went upstairs to evacuate the tenth to twelfth floors. I was glad the building was mostly empty this time of year, and since it was early afternoon, no one ventured in or out. Some neighbors had probably gone out for the day or were taking their afternoon nap. I hoped not many people would be asked to vacate their condos.

Only four people came out of the elevators, sent out of harm's way by the police, and they wandered out the back door toward the beach. I'd busied myself in front of the mailboxes, hoping to look as though I'd just come in. I didn't want anyone to question me about what was going on.

The police weren't up there more than ten minutes.

"The bomb squad is on its way," Mizenhimer said when they returned. "We'll have to ask you to wait here a while longer."

Within minutes, sirens wailing, an ambulance and fire truck arrived in the parking lot. Soon after, a van pulled up bearing the bomb squad and their equipment. Four men hustled into the lobby, one carrying a protective suit. Accompanying them, like a friendly dog, was a small tank-like robot with two mechanical arms and a camera mounted on it. After a brief discussion with Mizenhimer and his partner, the bomb squad and its mechanical mascot entered an elevator.

While they did whatever they did upstairs, Mizenhimer sat on a sofa and wrote up a report, and his partner guarded the front entrance to keep spectators away.

Again I waited anxiously as the minutes dragged on. Now I was beginning to regret that Mark wasn't around. At least he would be company. I could have used a hand holder at that point. But I knew that the fallout in terms of his anxiety over my well-being would not be a good trade-off. At last the bomb squad returned to the lobby.

One of the men carried several large Ziploc bags that held what looked like the contents of the envelope. He held them out to me and introduced himself. "I'm Corporal Sam Jones," he said. "Someone thinks of himself as a jokester. He'll find out how funny it is if we get our hands on him."

Contained in the bags were the envelope, wires, small travel alarm, and some other items I didn't recognize, along with a handwritten note that read, "Bang! You're dead!"

"We're taking this back to the forensics lab," he said and told me someone from CID would be in touch to question me about the incident.

I went back to my condo and wandered restlessly through its rooms. Even though the sender had not been there in person, my home had been violated. It may not have been a real bomb, but it had done its damage, psychologically if not physically. I wondered if I'd ever feel safe there again.

Within an hour, Caronis showed up at my door. After settling on my couch, he said seriously, "Mrs. Daniels, didn't I say to be careful? Have you been stirring up trouble?"

"If I have been, I certainly didn't mean to," I said in all sincerity. "Do you think this is Bud and Arnold's doing?"

"We might have to reconsider the assumption that they don't know of your involvement," he replied. "Of course, we're checking for fingerprints."

"What if they wore gloves?" I asked.

"I guess I'd be surprised. As I told you before, these guys aren't too bright. They're easily swayed by Packard, but they're not career thugs, so they're pretty unsophisticated when it comes to crime. And they probably don't even think of it as a crime. They're just doing 'the Lord's will.'"

"Well, I can't think of anybody else who would send it."

I really couldn't. I hadn't yet checked out Rachel, who had an opportunity to kill Gerry. After all, she could walk around the hospital, at will, without arousing suspicion. The Crafts From the Heart situation evidently had been resolved. And Maria's surprise at being caught seemed genuine. I don't think she was aware that Gerry had become concerned about the books.

Mark came home at suppertime, looking tired and discouraged. Evidently he had not had a good day, and I couldn't bring myself to add to his troubles by telling him mine. I didn't want him totally freaked out.

As we ate, he told me what had happened. "I don't know, Mom. It seemed like a good idea for me to come here, but Sarasota isn't exactly a Mecca for techies. And, again, the salary range pretty well sucks."

I wasn't going to get into another discussion on that subject. "So now what?" I asked.

"I set up several interviews in Tampa tomorrow. I've got to leave really early to make the first one."

"You'd better. The traffic on 75 can be bumper-to-bumper." That was true almost any hour of the day. I could only imagine what traffic must be like first thing in the morning. One of the great advantages of retirement is being able to stay off the roads during rush hour.

He went to bed early, setting his alarm for five. He assured me he could fix himself breakfast.

Mark was long gone by the time I got up. I tried to read for a while after breakfast, and when I couldn't concentrate on the words, I tried ironing. But I ended up scorching two blouses. My mind kept going back over the past few days, and nothing made any sense. I thought I should be doing something, but I had no idea what. Finally I decided to go to Sarasota Square Mall and shop. Maybe that would distract me.

I should have known better. I was too upset for shopping, and I'd been inside only a short while when it started to get to me. Seized by a sensation of vertigo brought on by the racks and racks of clothes crammed close together, I panicked. I was overwhelmed with a sense of drowning in a sea of blouses, skirts, and dresses, as if a multi-colored tidal wave were bearing down on me.

I escaped to my car and started driving aimlessly in an effort to shake off the feeling of impending doom. I realized that the accumulation of events had brought me to a point where I was becoming downright paranoid.

The only way to fight it was to be proactive, not reactive. I needed to do something positive, not just sit around and wait for disaster to happen.

After I calmed down a bit, I realized I was driving up Beneva, not far from Maria Alvarado's condominium. I wondered if it would do any good at all to talk to her again. I knew that her fate had not yet been decided by the members of the craft shop, and perhaps she would feel intimidated enough by the possibility of arrest that she might confide in me. I sincerely doubted that the group would want to prosecute her, but Maria had acted as though she expected the worst.

I hadn't been affected by her embezzlement, so she might consider me an ally. I sensed that, until we'd met with Maria, she'd been unaware that anyone had blown the whistle on her. Therefore, I considered her unlikely to want to wreak revenge on Gerry, but I wanted to verify that. She had not seemed to me like the kind of person who could lie easily.

I parked near her unit and went to the door. Her blue Ford was in her parking spot, so I assumed she was home. I rang the bell several times, but no one answered.

Just as I started to leave, the door in the next condo opened, and a middle-aged black woman stepped out to check her mailbox. Dressed in an aqua skirt, tailored white blouse, and heels, she looked as though she was about to go to work or go shopping.

"Hello, I'm Emma Daniels," I said, walking over to her front step. "Do you know if Maria is home? Her car's here, but she doesn't answer the bell."

The woman frowned. "I don't like the sound of that. Maria has high blood pressure, and she's blacked out a couple of times. I have a key to her house because we keep tabs on each other. Let me get it, and we'll see if she's okay."

The woman was back in less than a minute. "I'm Helen Lawson," she said as we hurried next door. "Maria and I have been neighbors for eight years."

I followed her as she unlocked the door and entered Maria's

house. Immediately inside the door, she let out an anguished cry and stopped so abruptly, I ran into her.

Alarmed, I stepped around her and saw the reason: Maria lay crumpled on the living room floor. A pool of dark reddish-brown blood had coagulated beneath her shattered head, and she clutched a gun in her outstretched hand. The smell of decay was in the air, and I had no doubt at all that she was dead.

Helen began to scream and kept screaming, the sound pounding my ears. The only reason I didn't faint dead away was because I felt the need to calm her, to somehow get her to quiet down.

I took her in my arms. "Shhhh," I said, "it's okay, it's okay." Of course, it obviously was not okay, but I was too stunned to say anything intelligent.

Finally she stopped, and her screams turned to deep sobs. She held me so tight, I could hardly breathe. By now, I was crying too. I couldn't believe it.

Why would Maria do this? I was sure the women from the craft shop would never prosecute her. I think they honestly wanted to help her. Surely she could have sensed that.

But the worst of it was my sense of guilt. Though I knew that Priscilla had been planning on checking the books even before I talked to her, maybe the fact that I'd said Arlene wanted to finish what her mother had begun had prodded the board into confronting Maria. They might have decided to overlook it otherwise. This outcome may have happened anyway, but I couldn't shake off my role in the tragedy.

I pulled away from Helen. She was still crying softly but seemed fairly under control now.

"We have to call 911," I said.

She nodded but didn't move. I could tell she expected me to do it. This was the second time in two days I'd been forced to call for help. The police were going to think I was like Typhoid Mary, bringing disaster wherever I went. My voice shook and cracked as I told the dispatcher what we had found.

As we waited for the police to arrive, I tried to get Helen to sit on the sofa, but she wouldn't budge. So we remained standing as far from the body as we could get in that small room.

"Did you hear anything that sounded like a gunshot?" I asked. The walls of their condos seemed about as soundproof as a piece of cardboard. If a gun had fired, she surely would have heard it.

"I didn't get home Monday till around midnight," she said, "and I took a sleeping pill last night because I've been bothered by insomnia lately. It probably happened while I was gone, or else I slept so soundly I didn't hear it."

The police arrived in about fifteen minutes. Ascertaining immediately that Maria was indeed dead, they radioed the homicide division. Helen and I huddled together in the corner of the living room while more officers appeared, along with men in suits.

One of the men introduced himself as Lieutenant Hale. While he interviewed us, the others spoke in low tones to each other as they took pictures of Maria's body and scoured the room for evidence.

Lieutenant Hale, his thin gray hair combed straight back from a high forehead, was a grandfatherly looking man with a patrician nose and a ruddy complexion. I figured him for a sailor, as so many were in this area.

"And how did you ladies happen to be here?" he asked.

I explained that I'd come to visit Maria, but I didn't tell him why. That all seemed unnecessary, now that she was dead. There was no need to tell the police that she was suspected of embezzling. Her case had been closed on that in the saddest possible way.

"I live next door," Helen explained. "When Emma saw that Maria's car was here, but she couldn't get her to answer the door, she was concerned. Since Maria had passed out a couple of times, she'd given me a key. I checked on her now and then if I hadn't seen her in a while. So I let myself in. . . ."

She broke down and began to cry again. I remembered I had a hankie in my purse and fished it out and gave it to her. She squeezed my hand in gratitude.

Hale asked her if she'd heard the gunshot, and she repeated what she'd told me.

"Neither of you have touched anything, have you?" he asked.

"Of course not," I said, rather miffed that he thought we'd be that dumb.

He then said we could go. "I may need to talk to you again," he added and took our names, addresses, and phone numbers.

We drifted out to the front step, still in shock. It was all so unreal, and I felt like I couldn't get a grip on things. Gerry's death had been quite another thing. I'd been told about it, but I hadn't seen her in death. To discover a body was something else again. I couldn't get the sight of Maria, lying on the floor with her head surrounded by a bloody halo, out of my mind.

"Why don't you come over to my house for a bit," Helen offered, sensing my hesitation. "Maybe it would help if we talked a little."

I wasn't sure I wanted to talk about it, but I knew I didn't want to be alone just yet. I nodded and followed her into her condo. White-cushioned teakwood furniture and colorful abstract paintings made an attractive arrangement in the small living room. Sunlight streamed through the clerestory windows.

"I was supposed to be on my way to work," she said, beckoning me to sit down. "But I'm going to call them and take a sick day. I've never been so sick about anything in my life. I can't believe she'd do that."

Helen excused herself and went into a bedroom to call. When she came back, she offered me tea or coffee.

I declined. "I think I might choke on anything I'd try to eat or drink right now," I said.

"I know how you feel," she agreed. "I find it inconceivable that Maria would commit suicide. For one thing, she was Catholic. A lapsed one, but nevertheless, I'm sure she still believed it was a sin to kill yourself. And I can't imagine what could be so bad in her life that would cause her to do such a thing. She always seemed upbeat." Helen shook her head to show it was beyond her imagining.

I debated whether or not to tell her about the embezzlement, finally deciding to do so to see what kind of response it would elicit. If she knew Maria well, perhaps she could throw a little more light on the whole business.

"What I'm going to tell you is in strictest confidence," I said. "Maria was accused of taking money from the craft shop where she worked."

"Maria? I can't believe it." Helen's disbelief seemed genuine. "She'd be the last person I'd suspect of that."

"She said she'd been sending the money to her mother in Cuba."

"But that's not possible!" Helen shot up off the sofa as if she'd been struck by lightning. "Maria's mother died years ago!"

CHAPTER · 9

AFTER LEAVING HELEN'S, I FELT AN URGENT NEED TO SEE CAL. I'D
never before dropped in on him unexpectedly, but I took the chance
he'd be home.

His neighborhood, in an older section of Sarasota, is full of
cookie-cutter houses, and most are a bit on the grim side: scruffy lots
with few if any trees, mildewed roofs, faded paint. But Cal's home
is like an oasis in the desert. He'd landscaped the yard with tropical
plants so thick, there's no room for lawn. Instead, the hibiscus, roses,
Gerbera daisies, and bougainvillea compete with the orchid tree
and tree of gold for the showiest color. He'd painted the small
stuccoed ranch the softest shade of beige and added red shutters
and doors. The whole effect is welcoming.

When I pulled onto his street, I noticed an unfamiliar car parked
in front of his house. What I wanted to discuss was not something
I wanted to share with strangers, so I decided to park at the end of
the block until the company left, hoping Cal wouldn't notice me,
should he come to the door. That would have been embarrassing; it
would look as though I was spying on him.

Twenty-five minutes later, just as I was about to give up and leave,
an attractive woman about my age opened the door and stepped
out onto the porch. Cal came out with her, and they embraced and
kissed before the woman got in her car and left.

Cal went back in the house, and I sat there in shock.

He and I had no "understanding." We'd never agreed to see each other exclusively. Good lord, we hadn't even been intimate. But I didn't realize until that minute how much he meant to me.

I pulled away, not even knowing where I was going. I drove around aimlessly, thinking about the good times Cal and I'd had together over the past few months. He'd never mentioned another woman, but why should he? He could easily be juggling two of us without either of us realizing it. Was that being deceptive? Not, I had to admit, unless we'd agreed not to see anyone else. And we certainly hadn't done that. I hated the jealousy that was eating away at me, but I couldn't will it away. I had to think about something different.

I decided to go to Crafts From the Heart and see if Priscilla was there. She needed to know about Maria, and it would be easier to hear it from me than to read it in the obituaries.

But when I walked in, I found that Catherine was tending the store. One of the triumvirate "board," she wore a tie-dyed shift that only added additional bulk to her already huge frame. She moved with surprising grace, however, as the folds of the material swirled about her like eddies in a stream.

"Hi, Emma," she said as I came in the door, "how you doing?"

I would have preferred to break the news to Priscilla, but Catherine could pass it along. There were no customers in the shop, so I went up to her and took her hand. "I'm afraid I have bad news."

She looked at me, startled. "What d'you mean?"

"Maria Alvarado is dead."

"What?" Her voice came out in a screech. "You can't mean it! What happened?"

I led her over to the round table, where the four of us had gathered to look at the books two days earlier, and sat down beside her. I had a hunch that Catherine was emotionally fragile, and I didn't want her freaking out on me.

"I stopped by to see her this morning," I said. I didn't explain why. "Her car was there, but she didn't answer the door. Her neighbor said she had a key to her house because Maria had passed out a couple of times. So we went in to check on her."

"And. . . ?" Catherine's eyes were wide, awaiting the punch line.

"We found her on the floor." I paused; the next part was hard to say. "She had a gun in her hand. She'd shot herself."

Catherine's mouth came open, but nothing came out for a few seconds. She looked like someone had slapped her. "Oh, no, no," she moaned. "Maria was such a sweetie pie. We must have pushed the darlin' right over the edge. We shouldn't have been so hard on her." She was absolutely stricken.

"Don't, Catherine," I said. "Don't blame yourself. I just learned something about Maria that puts a whole new light on things."

Her eyes got huge. "What're you sayin'?"

"Her next-door neighbor has known Maria for years. She says her mother is dead. Has been for a long time."

Catherine's mouth dropped open again, and she stared at me. "But . . . but . . . where'd all that money go, then?"

"I wish I knew. Did she talk about her mother a lot?"

"No. I don't recollect she ever mentioned her till the other day. She didn't talk much about her private life. But she was a dear, sweet lady. Always worried about other people's problems."

"Did she belong to a church?" I asked. Helen had said Maria was a lapsed Catholic, and I suddenly wondered if she'd joined One True Light Church. That could explain a lot.

"No. We talked some about our beliefs. She said she thought she could be a good Christian even if she didn't go to church. And it sure seemed like she was. She knew how much I fretted 'bout my weight, and she told me I should learn to love my body, no matter its size." Another tear slipped from her eye and rolled down to her chubby chin, where it hung unnoticed. "I'm tryin'," she said in a soft, sad voice.

I went to Dorrie's Lunchroom for a half-hearted bite of lunch. As I waited for my food, I tried to decide what to do next. But I couldn't concentrate. All I could think about was the woman who came out of Cal's house.

I suppose I'd neglected him recently. But after all, he'd told me he had to work on his article. An unexpected stab of fear grabbed my gut, almost as bad as the terror I'd experienced when I received the fake bomb. I didn't want to lose Cal. He was too special. I wasn't sure just what kind of a relationship I wanted. But I knew for damn sure I wanted him in my life.

I ate hurriedly and drove back to Cal's place. I didn't know what I was going to say to him, but I definitely wasn't going to mention seeing the woman. I'd never let him know I'd been watching his house. I guess I just wanted to see how he'd act toward me, certain I could sense a lack of enthusiasm on his part.

I knocked on his door, but there was no answer. I knocked a second time, without response. Finally, I walked down his driveway and peered through the garage window. His car was gone. A terrible emptiness swept over me.

At seven-thirty that evening, Mark came in acting pretty chipper for a change. Noticing that I'd made no attempt to prepare a meal, he suggested we go out to dinner.

"I had a couple of really good interviews," he said on the way to the restaurant. "It looks like something might work out for me in Tampa."

In spite of my unhappy state, I was delighted about that. If he lived in Tampa, he'd be just far enough away not to be monitoring my every move, but close enough for frequent visits. Mark tended to be oversolicitous of me, especially since his father died. If he knew what I was presently involved in, he'd probably have a heart attack.

"I should know by Friday," he said. "And I'm feeling so positive that at least one of them will work out, how about planning a celebration dinner for Friday night? Invite Cal along and make reservations at your favorite place. The sky's the limit."

"Consider it done," I said, my stomach flip-flopping at the mention of Cal.

As soon as we got home, I called Cal. I had a good excuse to talk to him now, without exposing my insecurities. But he didn't answer the phone. I left a message on his machine for him to call me, and tried unsuccessfully to still all the little doubts and worries echoing in my head.

The next morning Mark returned to Tampa for a second round of interviews. I sat at home waiting for Cal to call. Just before lunch, I called him once more, thinking that maybe his machine had malfunctioned. But, again, he didn't answer.

I had decided during the sleepless hours of the night that I needed to explain to Caronis the link between Gerry Stapleton and Maria Alvarado. So after lunch I drove to the police department.

The detective's greeting was, as always, unfailingly polite. I wondered when he was going to get tired of seeing me.

"I hope I haven't worn out my welcome," I began, "but there's something I thought you should know." I proceeded to explain the link between Geraldine and Maria. "It's probably pure coincidence," I concluded, shrugging my shoulders, "but I thought that should be your call, not mine."

He sat for several minutes without speaking, nodding his head, his thoughts far away. Finally, he leaned back in his chair and clasped his hands behind his head. "I'm glad you came. The connection may or may not be significant. Of course, yesterday when we tried to notify her next of kin, we learned that she had no living relatives."

"Do you think it was suicide?"

He looked me straight in the eye. "We're looking into that."

Well, I thought, *a little information is better than none at all.* "By the way," I said, "what about fingerprints on the fake bomb?"

"There were none."

"Do you think you'll ever find who sent it?"

"The chances are slim. The materials, the wrapping . . . everything was so generic, it gave us little to go on. On the other hand, if it had been the real thing, we might have had a better chance of finding the perp. It might have fit some MO, or we could have traced the ingredients. All the same, I hope you're still heeding the warning."

"I'm trying real hard to stay out of trouble," I said, deluding myself into believing that was the truth.

When I left the police department, I realized it had been a week since I'd visited Phil at the nursing home. I'd told Arlene that I would try to visit him regularly, and I wasn't off to a very good start.

At Brightwood I searched for the aide I'd talked to the week before, embarrassed that I hadn't even learned her name so I could ask for her at the desk. Instead, I strolled the halls until I saw her with a patient a few doors away from Phil's room. I waited until she came out, then went up to her with my hand outstretched.

"I'm sorry," I said, "I don't believe I got your name when I was here last week visiting Phil Stapleton."

She shook my hand, her smile as broad as ever. "Hey, Miz Daniels. I'm Theresa Sharp, but everyone calls me Tessie."

"How's Mr. Stapleton doing?"

"I'm real concerned. He don't want to get out of bed. I have to cajole him to eat. He's 'bout as low as he can get."

Poor guy. No wonder he was depressed. Who wouldn't have been, under the circumstances? "Have there been any more incidents like the one last week?"

"We keep a real close eye on him. So nothing's happened like that. But I was gonna call you tonight about something. Come on up to the desk."

I followed her to the nurses station, where she went behind the counter and searched through a stack of papers. She pulled out an envelope and handed it to me.

"Since I read his mail to him," she said, "I saw this before he did and put it away real quick before he could get a look at it."

The letter was addressed to him, the writing generated by a computer printer, and the postmark was from Ellenton, a town north of Sarasota. I pulled out the single sheet, a regular piece of typing paper folded into thirds. Inside, written in large bold letters, was the following: "I saw what you did to your wife. MURDERER! When they drag you into court, I'll be there to testify against you!" There was no signature.

What in the hell was that all about? If someone had actually seen him smother Geraldine, surely he or she would have told the police at the time. This letter could only be an attempt to frighten and intimidate Phil. It didn't seem to be an extortion letter; there was no demand for money in exchange for silence. Or would that come later? Maybe this was a warm-up to get him thoroughly intimidated and ready to cooperate.

But no sooner had I thought that than I discarded the idea. I was so sure that Phil was innocent, I didn't see how anyone could blackmail him. Until I realized that it was someone else's word against his. And now, he had no words at all.

"What should I do, Miz Daniels? Should I give this to the police?"

"I see them regularly. Why don't you let me take it to them?" That way, I would be doing my good citizen's duty and, at the same time, maybe scrounge another bit of information out of Caronis.

"That'd be good," she said, so I put it back in the envelope and stuck it in my pocketbook.

"Should I tell Miz Arlene about it when she calls?"

"It would upset her terribly. I wouldn't, at least for now."

"That's a relief. I sure didn't want to. I can just tell Mr. Phil's no more a murderer than the man in the moon. Why would somebody say such an ugly thing?"

Tessie and I were alike, there. Neither of us could know for sure that Phil didn't kill his wife, but we both would have bet our lives that he didn't. "Who knows why people do what they do? A twisted mind, I guess."

I went to Phil's room and found him asleep in his wheelchair. I didn't have the heart to wake him, so I sat there for twenty minutes, hoping he would rouse and see me. But he didn't. Sleep was an escape from the horrible reality of his life. I didn't want to interfere with this opportunity for a welcome respite, so I left.

As I walked to my car, I wondered who all might suspect that the police thought Phil had murdered Geraldine. Priscilla, for sure. God only knew whether she'd told everyone else at Crafts From the Heart. And it seemed possible, even probable, that the cops' suspicions had circulated amongst the hospital staff. Someone could have overheard the detective talking to Arlene. Or the results of the autopsy had gotten around, and people had drawn their own conclusions. What about members of One True Light Church? Rachel worked at the hospital. She could have heard the news and reported it to other church members. Any one of them could be using this knowledge to threaten, and eventually blackmail, Phil to make up for the money they lost in the lawsuit generated by his wife. And, of course, the staff at Brightwood. That was one heck of a pile of people.

Instead of going straight to the police station, I went by Cal's house instead. I knew I was acting like an adolescent, but I was becoming a little concerned. Was he mad at me for some reason? Had he gone out of town without telling me? Not that he was obligated to inform me of his every move. He normally talked to me every few days, however, and I hadn't spoken to him since Saturday.

His car was still gone. I sat in my car in front of his house for a few minutes, trying to assure myself that everything was okay. But so many awful things had happened lately, it was hard to keep my paranoia from taking over.

As I drove toward the police department with the letter Tessie had given me, the more I thought about it, the less I wanted to pass it along. This was one more thing that would solidify their suspicions about Phil. He didn't need that. After a few blocks, I'd made up my mind to hang onto it for a while, just until I'd cleared up a few things.

What I really wanted to do was to find out more about Rachel. Perhaps I could talk to Tom Guy if I could come up with some plausible excuse for asking questions about her. As I drove toward One True Light Church, I plotted my course of action.

The bell tinkled gaily as I opened the church door. As before, Tom Guy Packard appeared from a back room, pushing his oxygen tank before him. Perhaps it was the lighting, but his complexion seemed even sallower than before. His step faltered slightly. Even though it had been only a few days since I'd seen him, I could tell his health was failing rapidly.

"Oh, Mrs. Daniels," he said, his voice raspy and his breathing shallow. "How are you? Good to see you again."

I grasped his hand. "I'm fine, Reverend Packard. I hope you're doing well."

He shook his head. "Not too good, I'm afraid." He indicated a seat and sat down heavily on the adjoining folding chair.

"I'm sorry to hear that." What else can one say under such circumstances?

"The Lord's will be done. That's what I've always preached. I've had a good life. Now, tell me, to what do I owe this pleasure?"

"I met Rachel Greeson the day we cleaned up Rose Willis's house, and I understand that she knits beautiful sweaters. I'm involved with a local craft shop that is on the lookout for talented people, and I thought of her. But I couldn't find her in the phone directory, and I don't know how to get in touch with her." That much was true. There were a number of Greesons, and I didn't know her husband's name.

"Oh, yes, she's quite an expert knitter."

Tom Guy rubbed his knee in thought. I'd noticed he'd favored it some and probably suffered from arthritis, as well as emphysema.

"I think that would be a good outlet for her," he said. "And I'm sure she could always use the money. Families these days have a hard time making a go of it."

"Does she have children?" I wanted to find out as much as I could without asking questions that were too personal.

"Two—a boy and a girl. Nice kids. But you know how expensive it is to raise children," he said.

What does he mean by that? I wondered. My cynicism then took over. *Doesn't Rachel make a big enough pledge to the church?* "That's so true," I agreed. "Is there a Mr. Greeson?" Nobody had ever mentioned him.

"Oh, yes. Harold. He works in a vacuum cleaner store. I'm sorry to say, Rachel hasn't yet been able to convince him to join the church. But I know she's always trying to persuade him to save his soul. I'm sure she'll eventually be successful. And having strong faith can help ameliorate financial worries."

"Well, it sounds like she might welcome the idea of selling her work."

Tom Guy smiled for the first time. "I think you're right. Let me get her address for you. I'm pleased you want to do this."

"Would you do me a favor, Reverend? All this has to go before the board of directors. They'll need to see a piece of her work before making the decision to carry her sweaters. I'd appreciate it if you wouldn't say anything about it to her. We wouldn't want to get her hopes up, only to dash them. I will try to obtain a piece of her work without telling her why I want it."

"I won't say a word." He struggled to his feet. "Her address is in my office. I'll be right back."

A few minutes later, he brought me a card with Rachel's name, address, and phone number. I thanked him and watched for a minute as he shuffled slowly back to his office. I didn't think the Reverend Tom Guy Packard was long for this world.

CHAPTER · 10

SO FAR, ALL I'D LEARNED ABOUT RACHEL GREESON WAS HER ADDRESS and the fact that she had two children and a husband who sold sweepers.

How could I find out more? I knew it was possible to discover all kinds of information about people over the Internet, and Cal was just the person who knew how to do it. I drove home hurriedly to see if he'd returned my phone call. Hope springs eternal.

The first thing I did when I unlocked the door was check the answering machine. There were no messages.

I felt like I'd run out the string. I seemed to be going absolutely nowhere. Not as far as Gerry's death was concerned. Not in my personal life. Why didn't I just forget it and take up a hobby like knitting or watching soaps.

I put on my bathing suit and wandered along the water's edge down to Point of Rocks, where I could see the entire graceful curve of Crescent Beach glistening under the afternoon sun. I looked for shells, but it was too late in the day for that; the fine, white sand had been picked clean.

The rhythmic swoosh of the gentle surf and the chattering of the gulls gave me a feeling of peace that I'd lacked for some time. I vowed that I would take some time each day, from now on, to do this. It was vital; it somehow kept me sane.

I realized I was hungry—I'd eaten very little for lunch—so I returned to my condo to throw together a sandwich. The phone rang as I was spreading mayonnaise on the bread. It was Mark.

"Mom, great news. I've got a job offer. They want me to meet some guys first thing in the morning who are coming in from another branch, so it would make more sense for me to stay up here for the night rather than make that long commute. I can pick up a clean shirt and a razor and toothbrush here. I'll be at the Hyatt."

"That's wonderful, honey. What's the company? What's your job title to be?"

"It's a software company called Little River Technology. I'll be one of their programmers. They're really on the cutting edge, Ma. It's a great opportunity."

"I'll see you tomorrow night, then?"

"Depends on how late I'm tied up with them. I may need to stay over another night, so why don't we postpone the celebration dinner. We'll set a new time when I get back."

"That'll work. See you when I see you."

I hung up feeling that at least one small portion of my life was going well. I was truly thrilled for Mark. He sounded happier than he had in months. The well-being of your children—or lack of it—can have an enormous effect on your own peace of mind.

Since I wouldn't have to fix dinner for Mark and it was late afternoon, I made a small salad and ate it with my sandwich. I cleaned up the mess I'd made and carried out the trash.

When I returned from the Dumpster, I sat in the living room to watch the early local news. Halfway through the program, there was an urgent knock on my door. I peered through the peephole and saw Cal with an anguished look on his face.

I swung open the door. "Cal! What's wrong?" I was so glad to see him, and yet I was alarmed by his demeanor.

"Are you okay?" he asked as he enclosed me in his arms.

I pulled back. "Of course. Why wouldn't I be?" Here I'd been frantic over his disappearance for the past couple of days, and now he was in obvious distress over me. What was going on?

"I just got back from Fort Myers," he said breathlessly. "A message on my answering machine said you were in deep trouble. That's all it said." He took both my hands in his and clasped them tightly, as if afraid I'd slip away. "I didn't know if you'd been in an accident or what might have happened to you."

"I left you several messages. You should have known I was okay."

"This came after yours. And I tried to call you, but there was no answer."

"I took some trash out about twenty minutes ago."

"So that's where you were. I was out of my mind."

I held my arms out wide. "I'm fine. See? That must be somebody's idea of a joke."

"Well, it's one hell of a joke," he said and hugged me again.

As much as I hated the fact that he'd received such a shock, his reaction reassured me. Cal was genuinely upset that something might have happened to me. He let me go, and we sat down on the sofa.

"Did you recognize the voice?" I asked. "There were no specifics? Just that I was in trouble?"

"It was muffled, as if the person was deliberately disguising it. But it sounded menacing."

"Was it a man or a woman?"

"I couldn't even tell that. It was sort of a half whisper. What's going on? This call didn't come out of nowhere. They were obviously trying to scare me into getting you out of someone's hair. If I'm gonna get dragged into this kicking and screaming, you at least owe it to me to fill me in."

I couldn't deny that was true. And, frankly, I was to the point I needed to tell him. Not only for his help, but to feel someone was on my side. I was tired of going it alone.

So I told him everything that had happened since Saturday: the plot on the abortion clinic, the confrontation with Maria and her subsequent suicide, the fake bomb, the news from her neighbor that Maria's mother had long been dead. I told him about the letter that had been sent to Phil, but I didn't mention that I still had it.

The longer I talked, the more distressed he became.

"Good lord, girl, I'd say you've had more than enough warnings about poking around in this case. What do the police say?"

"They're concerned, but there's not much they can do. They've very little to go on to find who sent the fake bomb, but Caronis suspects it could be Bud and Arnold, the pair arrested in connection to the planned attack on the abortion clinic. But he doesn't seem to think the church members had anything to do with Gerry's death. Phil's still number-one suspect for that."

"I suppose the letter saying someone saw him do it put the final nail in his coffin, as far as the police are concerned."

I didn't know what to say. I wanted to gloss over it, make some noncommittal statement. But I couldn't do that with Cal. I valued our relationship, and I couldn't evade the truth with him. "I still have it."

He looked at me sternly, and again I felt like I was a fourth-grader about to be reprimanded by my teacher. "Why?" he asked.

"Because I think someone is trying to terrorize him. I don't think they saw him do anything. Almost everyone involved, from One True Light Church to the hospital staff, probably knows that the police suspect Phil and that he can't defend himself. I think it's meant to focus suspicion on him or to set him up for future blackmail."

"But, Emma, that's not for you to decide. It's up to the police."

I looked down at my hands and realized for the first time that they were balled up so tightly that my knuckles were white and my nails were digging into my palms. I was so tense, I was ready to fly apart. "You're right. I made a mistake. I'll take it to Caronis tomorrow."

Cal reached across and took my hand, disengaging my fingers one by one. It was like a caress. "Emma, you've got to be careful. I don't want anything to happen to you. Leave this to the professionals."

I could tell he was sincere in his concern. But I had to make him understand why I couldn't stop now.

"I need to find out who's doing this," I said. "How else can I protect myself? The intimidation isn't going to stop just because I opt out. They must think I know more than I actually do. And they're just going to keep after me and after me unless I stop them."

He looked at me a long time without speaking. I could almost see the wheels going around in his head. Was he thinking about giving me an ultimatum? We both knew he had no right to do that, as much as he may have wanted to.

Finally, he said, "Then you're going to include me in everything that's going on. If you're in danger, I want to know where you are and what you're doing. Otherwise, I can't deal with it."

It was an ultimatum of sorts. But one I could live with. It meant the world to me to know he cared that much.

"I need your help, then," I said. "I want to find out more about Rachel Greeson. Remember, she helped at Rose's house that day we were there? Well, I found out she has a job at the hospital. That would give her an opportunity to kill Gerry. I talked to Tom Guy about her—"

"For crying out loud, Emma," Cal interrupted, "no wonder you're in trouble."

"No, no," I protested. "I told Tom Guy that I'd learned that she knitted sweaters, which she does, and that I was connected to a craft shop that might be able to sell them for her."

"What if he finds out that was just a ruse for learning more about her?"

"He certainly seemed to buy my story."

Cal nodded his head in agitation. "Sure he did. Did it occur to you that this man is a consummate actor? How else could he persuade people the way he does? I think he has your number."

"I disagree. I think he bought it all."

Cal just shook his head and threw up his hands. "Whatever you say."

"Let's not argue over that. What's done is done. Will you do this for me, Cal? Will you find out what you can about Rachel? I'll write down her address and phone number for you."

I could see him struggle not to say something else, something he'd regret. He shrugged. "Sure. And you'll take the letter to the police."

He'd backed me into a corner. I'd have to do it.

Now that we'd covered all that territory, I had to ask the question. "Where've you been the past couple of days?"

"An old friend, Marge Kittrick, dropped by yesterday. Don't know if I ever mentioned her to you. She was a classmate years ago in Ann Arbor. She'd been visiting a mutual friend in Fort Myers and told me he's very ill with cancer. Not expected to live long. So I picked up as soon as she left and went down to see him. Stayed overnight to help his wife out with some business matters. What a downer. I knew Doug at the university. He was a big, strong man, even played a little professional football. You should see him now."

"I'm so sorry," I said as I hugged him. Sorry for Doug, sorry that I doubted Cal, sorry for the scare he had from the phone message. I'd do whatever I could to make it up to him.

Before I went to bed, I called Arlene. There was little I could tell her—much of what I knew would only alarm her—but I told her that I'd visited her dad that day and he seemed to be doing all right.

"Do you think the police are making any progress about who killed my mother?" she asked.

I wouldn't tell her that it seemed to me they weren't doing anything but focusing on her dad. I needed to leave her some semblance of hope. So I said, "I'm sure they're working on it."

"I really appreciate that you to kept me informed. I'd be a wreck if I didn't know what was going on."

You'd be a wreck if you did *know,* I thought. I hoped I could fix that.

CHAPTER · 11

I SLEPT A LITTLE MORE SOUNDLY THAT NIGHT, KNOWING AT LEAST that Cal had not abandoned me. If I'd learned one thing from all that had happened, it was to not take him for granted. Men like Cal are harder to find than an empty table at your favorite restaurant.

The next morning dawned rainy, something of an anomaly for autumn. Most of the time, the weather is pretty dry, and we'd had showers a week earlier. The rain dripped disconsolately down the windowpanes, signaling a miserable day. However, I wouldn't complain. Some of the flowers around our building looked a little faint of heart. The poor dears were thirsty, and our automatic sprinkler system missed the ones tucked back in the corners.

I'd promised Cal that I'd take the letter to Detective Caronis, although it was the last thing in the world I wanted to do. If I'd thought there was a possibility of lifting fingerprints from it, I could have drummed up some enthusiasm, but who knew how many people handled it at the nursing home besides Tessie and me. All it was going to do was deepen the cops' suspicions about Phil.

I decided to compromise. Rather than again confront Caronis's unspoken but nonetheless obvious disapproval of my involvement, I drove to the nearest post office, made a copy for myself on their copier, stuck the original in an envelope, and mailed it to the detective without adding a return address. He would think the nursing home staff mailed it to him after I supplied them with his name.

When I returned home, the phone was ringing as I unlocked the door.

"It's Cindy," the tearful voice at the other end of the phone said. "Is Mark there, by any chance?"

I couldn't believe it. As if life wasn't complicated enough. Why on earth was Mark's estranged wife trying to reach him? She'd left him for another man six months earlier, in a capricious move that had devastated him. I wanted her to be out of his life forever, but it would be another half year before he could file for divorce.

"What made you call here?" I asked, hearing the displeasure in my voice. She'd never gone out of her way to be gracious to me. She usually acted as though it was her unfortunate and onerous duty to simply be civil.

"I couldn't find him anywhere else, so I decided to take a chance." She was sniffling, and though she was twelve hundred miles away, I could tell she was pouting. She'd always seemed childish and self-centered to me, but I managed to keep my mouth shut about it around Mark.

"He *was* here," I said, unwilling to give her any details, "but he's gone right now, and I'm not sure when he'll be back." I didn't even offer to take a message.

She began to cry in earnest. "Oh, Emma, I don't know what to do," she sobbed. There was real terror in her voice, and I realized she was not putting on a show for me.

"What's the matter, Cindy?" I asked, having softened my tone slightly. I didn't want to get involved with her in any way, but there was such urgency in her crying that I couldn't just hang up on her.

"It's Frederick," she said reluctantly.

"Frederick who?" I was pretty sure I already knew the answer.

"The man I've been living with."

"And. . . ?" I found it difficult to be sympathetic.

"He's . . . I didn't know what he's really like," she said. "I've got to get away from him. Now!"

"Well, why don't you just leave?"

"He'll track me down anywhere I stay in town. I've got to leave Toledo. I'm terrified, Emma. There's no telling what he'd do."

This did shock me. I didn't give Cindy credit for having a lot of brains, but I never expected her to get herself into such a predicament. "What about getting a restraining order. Can't the police help you in some way?"

"No. I've already gone that route. It doesn't slow him down a bit." She broke into a new round of crying.

In spite of myself, I was beginning to feel sorry for her. "I don't know how to help you, Cindy. And Mark can't be reached right now. For that matter, I don't know what he could do, either."

"Could I come and stay with you for a few days? Just until I can figure out what to do? If I had anywhere else to go, I wouldn't think of asking." Though her own parents were alive and well, I knew they had been very disapproving of her behavior. I'm sure they wouldn't let her come home. Cindy thought I was the softer touch—which, of course, I am.

I hesitated. The last thing in the world I wanted was to have Cindy come visit. I knew that Mark would be furious when he returned from Tampa. A further complication was that I had only two bedrooms. They might still be married, but I knew they didn't want to share one. On the other hand, I didn't want it on my conscience if Frederick beat the hell out of her, or even killed her. What else could I do but tell her to come ahead? I'd have to figure out later how to work it out.

"Okay, Cindy, come on down. We'll just have to make the best of it. Let me know when your plane gets in. If I'm not here when you call, just leave a message on my machine."

"Oh, thank you, Emma. I can't tell you how grateful I am."

I'd never heard such gratitude in her voice before. She'd always held me at arm's length emotionally, and there'd been very little warmth in our relationship. Maybe she wasn't a completely cold fish, after all. But that didn't mean I was one bit happy about her coming to visit.

I hung up and wondered how to warn Mark. It would be just awful for him to walk in and find her here. But I didn't want to call Little River Technology when he was in the process of being introduced to his new employers. He'd be so upset over Cindy's arrival, he'd hardly be at his best. So I prayed her flight wouldn't be in till after he came back and I could prepare him.

I sat on the couch, staring at the streaks of rain running down the sliding doors that led to the balcony, trying to figure out sleeping arrangements. The couch was, in fact, a sofa bed that Paul and I had bought thinking we would have lots of visitors. But we never put it to use. We did have some company the first six months after we moved to Sarasota, but only one couple at a time, so the guest bedroom was adequate. The only visitor I'd had since Paul's death was Mark.

I had a feeling the mattress wasn't overly comfortable, and the sofa bed certainly didn't afford any privacy, but he would have to sleep on it. At least until he found living quarters in Tampa—which I hoped he was looking for now—or until Cindy left.

I thought of the irony of her leaving Mark. He may not have been a perfect husband, but I was positive he would never abuse a woman. How could she ever think she was improving her lot in life? Didn't she even have a hint beforehand that Frederick was a jerk?

Well, enough of worrying about Cindy and Mark. I needed to get my mind on something else. And the only thing that presented itself, of course, was Gerry's untimely death and who brought it about. I wondered if Christie Anne could tell me anything more about Rachel—personal things that Cal would never find in a computer file.

When I called her number, she answered the phone and agreed to meet me for lunch. I suggested we eat at Yoders Too, a Mennonite restaurant downtown, because she once had mentioned how much she loved their shoofly pie.

The rain had let up a little, but it was still sprinkling lightly when I left the building. At least the traffic on Siesta Key was light, since few people were headed toward the beach.

Christie Anne was waiting for me inside the door of the restaurant. She looked especially lovely. What I wouldn't have given for that gorgeous young complexion. Her white-gold hair, let loose from its usual ponytail, curled softly around her face.

She greeted me with a cheery hello, and we were immediately seated by a young woman who looked as though she'd stepped out of a history book. Her long dress and apron were nearly in style again, but the old-fashioned hairdo under the sheer white bonnet was definitely nineteenth century.

When I had once brought an out-of-state friend to Yoders Too, she said to the waitress, "I think it's so neat you're wearing a period costume." I'll never forget how red my friend's face turned when the girl smiled sweetly and said, "I'm Mennonite, ma'am." Sarasota has had a sizeable Mennonite community for years.

Christie Anne ordered chicken pot pie, and I ordered a salad, feeling conscientious for once. While we waited for our meals, we chatted about the weather and lack of traffic.

As an opener, I said, "Want to do Mobile Meals with me again next Tuesday? My helper won't be back in town yet." I hoped she would go to lunch with me afterward and I could delay my return home. I wanted to stay out of the house as much as possible if Cindy was going to be there.

"Sure, I'd love to. And, by the way, I'm going to start visiting other churches this Sunday. I've already made a list of about five I want to try out."

"That's a great idea, Christie Anne. Look them over carefully before you choose one."

She gave me a sheepish grin. "Don't worry. I'm gonna check 'em out real good this time."

"Say, um, changing the subject . . . would you mind if I pick your brain a little?"

She looked a little startled but said, "Okay."

"I'd like to know more about Rachel."

Christie Anne seemed troubled about my request. She folded and unfolded her napkin several times without looking at me. "I don't like to talk about other people," she said finally. "Particularly not their private lives."

"I wouldn't ask such a thing under ordinary circumstances. But this is very, very important. I can't explain it to you just now. Believe me, you could make a big difference by talking to me."

She looked skeptical. "You're sure. . . ?"

"I'm sure." Thank goodness she was young and reachable. Most people would have told me, in unmistakable language, what I could do with my questions.

Just then the waitress brought our meals, and Christie Anne took the opportunity to pretend to be absorbed in her chicken pot pie. I knew she was deciding what she should say.

At last, she spoke. "One thing I know for sure. Rachel hates being poor. She's always complaining that she can't afford to buy things she wants."

"What about her husband, Harold? Have you ever met him?"

"No, he doesn't belong to the church. Seems funny, since she's so devoted to Reverend Packard. I think she keeps trying to get him there, but so far, he won't come. I sometimes wonder what it is she sees in him. I've heard other people say he's kind of a jerk, but she doesn't seem to see it that way. Every once in a while, she'll brag on him . . . like the time he won two hundred dollars in the lottery. You'd think it took special brains to do that."

"What about her kids?"

"Chris is eight and Katie is nine. They're kind of pitiful, seem afraid of their own shadow. I used to teach Sunday School at One True Light and had them in my class. But they were so shy, they hardly ever said anything. I tried to bring them out, but they never wanted to join in. It's sad to see little kids like that."

"Do you have any idea why they're like that?"

She looked at me for quite a while, as if deciding whether to share her thoughts. "Promise you'll never repeat this to anyone?"

"Of course."

"I always thought maybe they were mistreated. When I was growing up, I had a friend who got beat up. She acted the very same way."

"Who do you think did it? Rachel or Harold?"

"I couldn't say. Maybe one or the other, or both. At the very least, someone probably yelled and screamed at them, and that's why they're so insecure. Once, when one of their classmates had a cast on his arm, Chris boasted that he'd had a broken arm when he was a couple of years old. To tell you the truth, I don't think he really remembered it. Probably saw pictures of himself with a cast, or heard about it. But I always wondered if his dad or mom did it."

Noticing how troubled she appeared, I asked, "Did anyone from the church ever report it to authorities?"

She shook her head. "There just wasn't enough to base it on. If the kids had bruises, they were where they didn't show. It's just awful to worry so about little kids and not be able to do a thing about it."

Christie Anne had almost finished off her pot pie, and I'd barely begun my salad, so I dug in.

"Well," she continued, "I'm not absolutely sure one of the parents did that to Chris. Maybe it was just an accident. I'd like to think so, anyway."

Our waitress came and took Christie Anne's spanking clean plate. "Dessert?" she asked, handing us back the menus.

"I'll pass," I said, handing my menu right back, not daring to allow myself to be tempted by the long list of homemade desserts, "but I think she wants shoofly pie."

"Yeah!" Christie Anne agreed, grinning ear to ear.

I ordered coffee and she ordered another coke.

"Can you tell me anything about Rachel's job?" I asked after the waitress left.

"I think she works in the housekeeping department at the hospital. From everything she's said, I don't think she makes much money."

"Since she complains about being poor."

"Yeah. Champagne tastes on a beer budget. My dad always uses that expression."

The waitress delivered Christie Anne's shoofly pie as I finished up my salad. I wanted a piece so much, I could have cried.

"Here, try it," she said graciously, pushing the plate across the table toward me.

Was my longing that obvious? I certainly couldn't hurt her feelings by refusing. It tasted like ambrosia, melting in my mouth. One bite was enough to take the edge off my desire.

"What else do you know about Rachel?" I asked, watching her savor every mouthful, her expression one of near rapture. "Any hobbies, interests? Other than the knitting you told me about." I was afraid she was going to wonder why I persisted in asking questions, but her attention was riveted on the pie.

"She's always talking about how she's going to win the lottery, big-time. It's like a fixation or something." Christie Anne toyed with the last little morsel, as though she might never have another piece of shoofly pie in her entire life.

"Well, lots of people dream that," I said.

"Exactly. But the most I ever heard that either of them won was Harold's two hundred bucks."

"Anything else?"

"Not really. She's real involved in One True Light. I think the church is sometimes the only thing that keeps her going. She darn near worships the ground Reverend Packard walks on."

That did not surprise me. But it made me wonder what Rachel would be willing to do in Tom Guy's name.

Christie Anne had little else to add about Rachel. We noticed that a long line had formed in the vestibule, so we decided we'd better not hold up the table any longer.

We parted ways after agreeing that I'd pick her up on Tuesday to drive the Mobile Meals route. I was becoming more and more fond of Christie Anne. My first impression had been that she was immature and not all that intelligent. But the more I saw her, the more I realized she was a bright and thoughtful young woman.

CHAPTER · 12

WHEN I GOT HOME, THE MESSAGE LIGHT ON MY MACHINE WAS blinking. I couldn't believe such an innocuous little red light could fill me with dread.

It was Cindy. She wasn't coming till the next morning. She needed to tie up some loose ends and would be in Sarasota by eleven-thirty. In the meantime, she was hiding out in a motel.

I guess the message could have been far worse. At least now I'd probably have time to warn Mark she was coming, although I knew that was going to be one rough conversation. I hoped he had found a place to stay in Tampa and could be out of here before she came.

Cal called me later in the afternoon. "I haven't been able to come up with much about Rachel Greeson," he said. "There's more about her husband, Harold. He's been arrested several times. Apparently he likes to fight—he has two arrests for assault and battery."

"Was that for beating up Rachel?"

"No, these were bar fights. I found little blurbs in the *Herald-Tribune* back issues. And in the police reports, I found a charge of passing bad checks."

"He sounds like a real winner. Nothing on Rachel?"

"A baby-sitter once took her to small claims court. Apparently, Rachel stiffed her on her paycheck. This was some years ago."

"Hmmm. Did it give a name?"

"Yeah. Lottie Turnbull." He read an address on Fourteenth Street.

From the number, it sounded like it would be in the area just north of downtown.

"Look," he said, "it's been a while since we've done anything but talk about this mess. How about going out to dinner with me, and we'll talk about something else for a change?"

"I'd love it."

"Pick you up at six?"

"Great."

I've never spent a lot of time with makeup and hairdos and all that stuff. Paul had been the impatient kind. When he wanted to go somewhere, he wanted to go *now*, and he wasn't about to wait while I applied eyeliner or foundation or whatever. So I went for the "natural look," which suited me fine at the time. But now, at age fifty-seven, natural wasn't all that great. I watched in dismay as the wrinkles increased and deepened, the eyelids sagged, the chin fell, and the jowls drooped.

I'd recently gotten one of those free makeup demonstrations from a department store, and occasionally, when I thought about it and wasn't too busy, I tried to duplicate what I'd learned. So before Cal arrived, I spent twenty minutes carefully applying all the various products I'd purchased that day.

Assessing the results carefully in the mirror, I decided I didn't look too bad for an old broad. Of course, I knew perfectly well that the lotions and powders didn't really make that much difference. But there must be something about going through the motions that releases endorphins, because I felt pretty good.

Cal came right on time, as always. He looked pretty nifty in my favorite outfit of his, navy blue sport coat and gray slacks with a wild and snazzy paisley tie. His hair was especially wavy in the humid weather, and little tendrils curled along his neck.

The only thing to spoil the image was the grungy walking cast, which had become pretty shopworn, even though he had a little "bootie" with Velcro closures to wear over it.

"Lookin' good, Ms. Daniels," he said.

So all my effort paid off, after all.

"Look pretty smart, yourself. But I bet you're tired of that thing," I said, gesturing toward his foot.

He sighed. "Pain in the ass, though it could be worse. But, remember now, we're talking only about positive things tonight."

"Yes, sir." I saluted. "How's this for positive? I got an interesting Zinfandel recently, so I fixed some crudités and cheese cubes to have before we go. No jokes about my hors d'oeuvres, though." I don't go in much for the fancy stuff. Carrot sticks and store-bought dip are about my speed.

"Wouldn't think of it," he said. "Anybody who goes to the trouble to feed me won't get any static from me."

We sat on the balcony and admired the view as we drank our wine. This was going to be a wonderful, relaxing night; I could feel it in my bones. When our glasses were empty, we decided to leave.

"Where do you want to go?" he asked as we descended to the lobby in the elevator.

"How about the Hideaway?" I suggested, since we both like the small, unpretentious seafood restaurant at the far end of Anna Marie Island.

"Great. I'm hungry for some crab cakes."

Cal had pulled into a guest space near the door of my condo building, and as we walked toward his car, I could tell something didn't seem right about it. A shadow quickly fell across my day, a gut feeling that maybe things weren't going to be so relaxing after all. As we got closer, it became evident what was wrong. All four tires had been slashed, and the metal wheel rims sat almost on the ground atop ruined rubber.

"Oh, no!" I grabbed Cal's hand for support.

He stood stock-still, his expression one of controlled fury. "Damn," he said in a low voice. He pulled a cell phone out of his pocket. "I'm calling the police. Should I ask for Caronis?"

"No, his shift would be over. And it likely has nothing to do with what's been going on."

"You really believe that?" he asked, incredulous.

"Well, it's your car, not mine. It's probably just the work of vandals, a random act. Anyway, that's what the police would say."

"Yeah, you're right. What do you say we go on to supper and call it in when we get back? I don't think it'll make much difference. It'll have to be towed, and I can take a taxi home. And, frankly, I'm hungry."

"That works for me." I wasn't about to protest. I'd been hungry since about an hour after my salad lunch.

As we walked toward my car, Cal took my hand and gave it a squeeze. "Never-ending, isn't it?"

"It sometimes seems that way."

As we approached my parking space halfway down the second row of covered carports, Cal's steps slowed almost to a halt.

"What's the matter?" I asked.

"I'm not sure," he said, stopping altogether. "I just have this feeling that something's wrong."

"Wrong how?"

He shook his head. Then he took off his sport coat and handed it to me. "Hold this a minute, will you?" He walked over to my Civic and knelt down beside it.

"Cal?" I said, wondering if he'd lost his mind. I couldn't imagine what the blacktop would do to his gray slacks.

Without a word, he lay down on his back and inched headfirst under the car. All I could think of was the oil spot under there that had accumulated, drip by drip, over the years. His shirt would be ruined.

Within five minutes he scooted back out again and struggled to his feet, not an easy thing to do with the cast. Traces of grease covered his white shirt, and he looked very sober. "Let's go back to the lobby right now. We have to call the cops."

"What did you find?" I began to realize what was going on. My knees felt as though they couldn't quite hold me up, and I put my hand out and held onto the side-view mirror to steady myself.

"Looks like a bomb under there."

Cal called 911 on his cell phone and made me wait in the lobby of the building. He stood out front and made sure no one else walked or drove near my car till the bomb squad got there. The whole scenario was much more public this time, since it all played out within view of Midnight Pass Road. An ambulance and fire truck came roaring up. A cop kept cars from pulling into the drive, which probably ticked off some residents trying to get home, but the authorities didn't want anyone blown to kingdom come. All I could think of was that the condo association was going to have me drummed out of La Hacienda. They might tolerate one time. But twice?

It was seven-thirty before the bomb squad finished their job, all out of sight from where I sat in the lobby. By that time, Caronis had been notified and was there to talk to us. When we thought it was just kids slashing the tires, it didn't warrant his attention. But this bomb couldn't have been the work of pranksters, and was a much more serious matter. Detectives, like doctors, can be on call at all hours when lives are at stake.

"So," he greeted me as he walked in the front door of La Hacienda. I didn't have a clue whether he was mad at me or sorry for me.

I reintroduced him to Cal, considering it had been some months since they'd met for the interview, and suggested it might be more comfortable to talk in my condo.

"Would it be okay if I ordered a couple of pizzas?" I asked as I unlocked my door. "We were on our way out to dinner." In spite of all that had happened, my stomach was growling like crazy. And I'd been through the bomb routine once before. This was probably a dud, too.

"Be my guest," Caronis said magnanimously. "I personally like anchovies and olives," he added with a wink.

So maybe he wasn't upset with me, after all. I ordered two large pizzas, one with onions and peppers, which I knew Cal liked as much as I did.

After I began brewing a pot of coffee, we sat down around the dining table in anticipation of the pizza delivery.

I couldn't stand the suspense another minute. "So what exactly did they find under my car?" I asked.

"A real bomb this time. Starting the car would have detonated it. It very well could have been lethal."

I looked at Cal and he looked at me. At that moment I didn't have much appetite. We had come so close. It was all I could do not to excuse myself and go retch in the bathroom, but I was determined to keep a cool front for Caronis.

Then we settled down to the interrogation. Cal took the lead and described how we found his tires slashed.

"How long were you in the building?" the detective asked.

"Couldn't have been more than forty-five minutes. We had some wine and cheese before we left to go eat."

"Did you see anybody around when you drove in?"

"No. Emma has probably told you that the building isn't very full this time of year. So I don't often run into other people here during the off season. Someone could have been out in the lot, skulking around, but I didn't see anybody."

"Did you observe any activity when you came out of the building?" He directed this question to us both.

We shook our heads.

"The only thing I noticed," I said, "was that Cal's car didn't look quite right. But I couldn't figure out what was wrong till we were almost next to it."

"Me too," said Cal. "I certainly wasn't expecting anything to happen to my car, so it took me a minute to realize that the tires had been slashed. I thought it was some kind of monstrous prank, kids out raising hell."

"What made you look under Emma's car?"

Cal stared at the ceiling for a minute, tapping the table with his fingers. He looked again at Caronis. "Maybe women aren't the only ones who have intuition. As we walked toward her car, I was thinking about the threats and the fake bomb that had been sent to her. It occurred to me that someone might have seen me, realized I was here to pick up Emma, and wanted to make sure we took her car rather than mine. And that meant they'd done something to her car."

Caronis nodded gravely. "And who might that be? Who would recognize you and connect you with her?"

We both were stumped for a minute. Not many people knew about our relationship. We occasionally passed other tenants in the building and spoke, but I'd never introduced Cal to any of them except my next-door neighbors, who were gone. And I couldn't imagine any of the neighbors having murderous thoughts toward us.

"Oh, I know," Cal said. "Last Saturday, the two of us worked with members of One True Light Church to fix up a woman's home that badly needed repair. Emma had asked Reverend Packard if some of his parishioners could help."

"Why Reverend Packard?" Caronis turned to me. He already knew about this, of course. I'd reported the overheard conversation about the planned attack on the abortion clinic. But I guess I'd failed to tell him that the project at Rose's house was my idea.

I knew *he* knew why I'd done it, but he wanted me to spell it out. "Because I knew that Geraldine Stapleton had sued them over blockading the abortion clinic. I just wanted to meet them, see what they were like."

Caronis was nodding now with a slight smile on his lips as though I'd finally spilled the beans. "So your involvement with them came from an ulterior motive. You thought the police department wasn't taking enough interest in them, so you decided to find out what you could on your own."

"Something like that," I said sheepishly.

"Who all worked with you that day?"

"Reverend Packard, Christie Anne Griffin, Rachel Greeson, Arnold Shafner, and Richard Thompson. There were three other men, but I can't remember their names now. I never really talked to them."

"Uh-huh," said Caronis. "That's where you overheard Bud and Arnold talk about the butyric acid attack they were planning on the clinic. Real upstanding citizens, those two."

"Well, I didn't actually overhear them," I said. "My son, Mark, did."

"Did you ever tell him the outcome of the investigation?" Caronis asked, probably knowing full well I didn't want to worry Mark.

I glanced at Cal, who was looking pretty grim, and then back at the detective. "No," I said quietly.

"That's what I figured," he said. "What about the women who were there?"

"I'm sure Christie Anne had nothing to do with it. I've gotten to know her pretty well, and she had no idea what was really going on in that church. She's left it now. Rachel Greeson is another matter. All I know about her is she worships Reverend Packard, and some people think her kids might be abused, but they have no concrete evidence."

I gave him her address, and he wrote it down in a little black book he took from his pocket.

Just then the doorbell rang. The pizza delivery man had arrived.

"I guess this is what is known as comfort food," I said, setting the boxes on the dining room table. "Doesn't quite make up for the crab cakes I missed out on, but when under stress, pizza's a pretty good substitute. Shame it ends up as extra pounds around your middle and your derrière." I realized I was babbling on like an idiot, but I wanted to deflect the conversation to another topic.

Cal reached over and patted my hand. "To heck with the pounds. Just be thankful you're alive." So much for going for the small talk.

"He's right," added Caronis, helping himself to two slices. "If Cal hadn't come to take you out tonight, you wouldn't have had a clue that anything was wrong with your car. He was in the right place at the right time."

I hadn't thought of it that way. My hand started shaking as I thought how close I'd come to being blown to smithereens. My appetite deserted me, and I only nibbled at my pizza while the men wolfed theirs down. Evidently Cal wasn't as easily intimidated as I was.

We were still sitting around eating when Mark suddenly came through the door about eight-thirty. I'd temporarily forgotten about him. Since I hadn't heard from him again, I should have expected him that night.

He stopped in his tracks when he saw the three of us sitting around the table. "Well, hello," he said hesitantly.

Cal got up and offered his seat. "Have some pizza with us, Mark," he offered.

Caronis stood up as well. I sorely wished that he'd already left.

"Mark, this is Detective Caronis," I said, inwardly wincing.

"Hello, sir." Mark shook his hand. "I hope this is a social visit."

"Not exactly." Caronis waved toward the table in an effort to lighten things up. "But your mom invited me to eat with her and Cal. Why don't you join us? There's plenty."

Mark stared at me. I could almost see huge question marks hovering around his head.

"I'll fill you in later," I told him, giving him my now's-not-the-time-to-discuss-it look. "Aren't you hungry?"

Mark's gaze went from Cal to Caronis to me. I could tell he didn't like the situation one bit. "I ate before I left Tampa. Thanks anyway." He was still wearing a business suit, dress shirt, and tie.

"Why don't you get into something more comfortable?" I said, trying to get him out of the room, if at all possible.

Without a word, he picked up his briefcase and went into the bedroom and shut the door.

I leaned over and spoke in a low voice to Caronis. "He's going to be upset over this. I'd like to tell him in my own way, after you've gone, if you don't mind."

"Well, if you don't think he can add anything—"

"He's been out of town for the past couple of days. He knows nothing because I haven't told him anything. He tends to worry, on general principles, anyway, and he has enough on his mind without stewing about me."

Caronis took a napkin and wiped his mouth. "I guess it's time for me to go, then." He scooted back his chair and shook Cal's hand again. "I'm having both your cars taken to our impound lot. Want to see if we can find any prints or trace evidence on them."

"Will you have to keep them very long?" I asked, upset that I'd be without my little car, though I knew I could never again blithely jump into the driver's seat and take off, without many reservations.

"A few days. I'll let you know when you can get them."

After the detective left, Cal finished off his last few bites and said, "I'll call a cab."

"Why don't you stick around? I think it would be easier to tell Mark if you're here."

"Are you sure?"

I nodded.

I planned to tell Mark about the bomb now. I'd save the part about Cindy till later. I wondered which piece of news would upset him most.

CHAPTER · 13

MARK CAME OUT OF THE BEDROOM ABOUT FIFTEEN MINUTES LATER, dressed in shorts, polo shirt, and sandals. Cal had helped me clear off the table, and we sat on the couch, waiting for him.

Mark settled down opposite us, looking very concerned. "Okay," he said. "Tell me what's going on."

Cal was determined to make light of it. "We seem to be having a little car trouble."

"Mom?"

What could I do? I knew I couldn't wiggle my way out of it. "Cal found a bomb under my car."

There was a moment of stunned silence as he took this in. "This is a joke, right?"

I tried to appear calm and unruffled. Cal squeezed my hand in support.

"I was just trying to help a friend," I said.

"That doesn't make one damn bit of sense." Giving me a look that could have frozen the Gulf of Mexico, Mark stood up and started to pace. He was extremely agitated. "Well, are you going to tell me the whole story?" he growled, stopping only a moment to speak before resuming his nervous marching.

"I'll try, if you'll only sit down," I said.

He stalked back to the chair and dropped into it.

I tried to make it short and sweet. I explained about Geraldine and Phil, and gave him a brief rundown of Gerry's problems with Tom Guy Packard. I didn't see the point in bringing up Crafts From the Heart and poor Maria. Nor did I mention the fake bomb I'd received in the mail. He would have been furious that I didn't tell him about it at the time.

"So that's why you asked members of his church to clean up that woman's house. I thought it was a little strange. You were scoping him out, weren't you?"

I had to admit I was.

"Wait a minute," he said. "I told you some guys were talking about the abortion clinic. Do you know what that was about?"

I nodded. "I passed it along to the police, and they found out that they were planning a butyric acid attack. See, if you hadn't heard them, the cops wouldn't have been able to prevent it."

"And you wouldn't have bombs under your car." Mark had become very somber.

"Maybe not," Cal spoke up. "Caronis made sure that they didn't know your mom was responsible for their arrest."

"Oh," Mark said sarcastically, "so it's just some random killer out there who happened to pick out your car. What a coincidence."

"Calm down, Mark," I said. "I'm going to be fine."

"Providing you don't leave the house."

"I don't intend to be a prisoner in my own home. I'll be extremely careful."

"Promise me you won't drive till they catch whoever did it."

"Well, they towed my car to check for evidence, so I'll not be driving it for a while."

"Take a cab when you go out. I'll pay for it, if you can't afford it."

I went over to his chair and crouched down in front of him. I held his hand and patted it gently. "I'll be okay, Mark. I can take care of myself. Please don't get so upset over it."

He appeared to be on the edge of tears. "I can barely handle losing Dad. I don't know what I'd do if anything happened to you."

"Honey, I'm going to be just fine. Don't be such a worrywart."

"I should have gotten a job here in Sarasota so I could keep you out of trouble," he said. "If only I'd known what kind of foolishness you'd be getting yourself into."

I stood up before my legs turned to stone. "I don't mean to upset you. But I am a grown woman, and it is my life."

"You still need a keeper."

That angered me. "I'm not some zoo animal, you know."

"I was just kidding, Mom."

Like hell he was.

After Mark had calmed down, Cal called for a cab and went on down to the lobby to wait for it. That meant I had another confession to make to my son, and how I dreaded it. To postpone that awful moment, I asked him about his new job, hoping to elicit a more cheerful mood.

"I think I'm going to like it a lot," he said. "My job is interesting. I like everyone I've met so far. I think it's just the ticket for turning my life around. I can't tell you how glad I am to be out of Toledo. I want to forget the past."

Oh, terrific. I was just about to dredge it all up again.

"Have you found a place to live?" I asked, hoping against hope.

"Haven't had time yet. They told me to take a couple of days next week to find an apartment."

"I see." How was I going to tell him? Should I wait till morning? One of my worst habits is postponing unpleasant things until the last possible minute. But I decided he'd be even madder if I did that. There was nothing to be done but come clean.

"Mark . . . honey. . . ."

His eyes narrowed. "I know that tone and I don't like it. What do you have to confess now?"

"I got a call this morning."

"Okay."

"It was Cindy."

His face got very red. "What the hell is she bothering you for?"

"Her boyfriend is beating her up."

"Too bad!" He said each word with great emphasis, then put his head in his hands and shook it slowly back and forth. Then he looked up at me. "Am I supposed to care?"

"She's frightened, Mark. I think she's afraid he might kill her."

"Aw, Mom, she's just looking for sympathy. He probably dumped her, and now she's out on the street. She always was the little actress, exaggerating everything."

"I don't think she was making it up. She was darn near hysterical. She says she has to get out of town. I told her she could stay here for a few days." I braced myself for his reaction.

Good thing I did.

He was furious, pounding on the end table with his fist, causing the lamp to dance around as though we were having a mild earthquake. "Dammit, I don't believe it! How can you do that?"

"I didn't want it on my conscience if he killed her. I felt I had no choice."

"When's she coming?"

"Tomorrow. About eleven-thirty. I'm going to pick her up at the airport."

"First thing, then, I'm outta here. I'll go back to Tampa tomorrow and find an apartment. I refuse to stay anywhere near that woman."

"I thought you could sleep on the sofa bed."

"No way. I refuse to stay in the same house. Let me know when she's gone, so I can visit you."

I sighed and gave up the argument. "Okay, Mark, do what you must. I'm sorry it upsets you so, but I had to let her come."

He got up and walked toward the bedroom. "I'll get my things packed so I can leave early in the morning."

Now I knew what it meant to be between a rock and a hard place. Mark's heart was like a rock, and Cindy had put me in a hard place—right between the two of them.

True to his word, Mark took off at eight the next morning. He was a little more subdued, but he still wasn't happy about the situation.

I'd gotten up to cook him a substantial breakfast of bacon and eggs and hash browns. I guess that's the way mothers have tried to smooth things over since Day One.

"Don't let her take advantage of you," he said as he concentrated on buttering his toast. Then he looked up at me. "Oh, hell. She already has. Just don't let it go on and on."

"I don't think she's any more eager to be with me than I am to be with her," I said. "I must have been her very last resort."

After Mark left, I called and arranged for a rental car to be delivered. I knew he wanted me to take taxis, but that was too expensive, even if he said he would pay for it. I'd park it somewhere other than my assigned parking space and try to make sure no one saw me get in and out of it at my building.

They delivered a bright red Focus. Even though I had always wanted a red car, I wished it had been a more neutral color, one that wasn't so eye-catching, since I was trying to keep a low profile. I took the delivery boy back to the rental agency, and they said they had nothing but bright-colored cars in the subcompacts. It seems like the smaller the car, the wilder the color. Maybe that's supposed to make up for lack of comfort. I couldn't afford to get a bigger car, so I kept it.

I dropped by the supermarket to stock up on some groceries for Cindy. By the time I'd taken them home and put everything away, it was time to head for the airport.

I met her at baggage claim. I was shocked at how thin and haggard she looked. Always slender, she took great pride in her size-six figure. But now she appeared almost skeletal, her clothes hanging loosely on her frame. Her once-pretty auburn hair had lost its sheen, and appeared dirty and stringy. That was so unlike her; she'd been meticulous about her appearance before she separated from Mark.

And I could detect traces of old bruises under her eyes and on her chin.

"Hi, Emma," she said, trying for a smile but not quite making it. She'd already retrieved two suitcases from the conveyor belt, and my spirits sank at the sight of them. It looked like she planned to stay a while.

"Ready to go?" I asked.

She nodded, and we each rolled a suitcase out to the parking lot.

"You must have gotten a new car," she said as she settled into the passenger seat.

"No, this is a rental," I said. "It's a long story, and I won't bore you with it."

She was quiet all the way out to Siesta Key. That was not unusual, since she'd never been very chatty with me. Before she separated from Mark, the silence had seemed more like a deliberate slight, while this time I reasoned that she was too emotionally exhausted to be sociable. Or was everything the same, and only my perception had changed?

Once we got home, I fixed some sandwiches and iced tea and suggested we eat on the balcony. I thought the view of the beach might cheer her up. It always works for me.

As much as I didn't want her staying in my home, I couldn't find it in me to be ungracious. Maybe that's my old-fashioned upbringing. I tried to draw her into a conversation, if only to be polite. And to find out what she intended to do. "So what are your plans, Cindy? Are you taking vacation, or have you left your job?"

"I quit," she said, pretending to be absorbed in stirring sugar into her tea. "Frederick works there, you know. It was impossible to stay with him around."

This was not good news. Did she expect Mark to support her? Was she going to look for a job in Florida? Each possibility seemed worse than the last.

"I've got to decide what to do," she continued. "I've got some vacation pay coming, so I'm all right for a couple of weeks."

A couple of weeks? I'd thought she'd stay a couple of days. I wondered again how I always managed to get myself into situations like this.

"Where's Mark?" she asked. "Is he in Sarasota?"

"He has a new job in Tampa, Cindy. He's up there looking for an apartment right now."

"Oh." She looked disappointed. "Does he have plans to come down here at all?"

"I don't believe so," I said. *Not as long as you're here,* I thought.

"I don't suppose you have a telephone number for him."

"I sure don't," I said, relieved I didn't have to lie.

Our conversation fizzled out after that. After we finished eating, I said, "I have to run some errands, Cindy. Why don't you lie down or take a walk on the beach?"

"Can I come with you?" Her voice sounded like the pleading of a small child, plaintive and desperate.

"I don't think—"

"Emma," she interrupted, "I can't stand to be alone. My nerves are just shot. I'll not bother you. Please let me come."

So that's how she wanted it. Cindy obviously was determined to follow me everywhere, whether I liked it or not. I could only pray that my little shadow didn't plan to stay the full two weeks.

I gathered up my plate and glass to take to the kitchen. "I have some private business to take care of, Cindy," I said. "I can't ask you to come in with me."

"I'll sit in the car and wait for you, then."

"Well, okay. But I think you'd be much happier on the beach than sitting in a hot car."

There was no answer. She'd made up her mind.

After we cleared up, we got the car from the guest space where I'd parked it and headed back into Sarasota. I'd decided I wanted to talk to Lottie Turnbull, the baby-sitter who'd sued Rachel Greeson for back pay. I didn't know what she could tell me, but I hoped she might know something significant. Several years had passed since the lawsuit, so when I looked in the phone book earlier that morning, I'd been pleasantly surprised to see that she still lived on Fourteenth Street. I'd called and asked her if I could meet with her at two, and she'd agreed.

I took a circuitous route through downtown to show Cindy some of Sarasota's landmarks, since the only other time she'd been in town was for Paul's funeral. She perked up somewhat.

"Pretty nice place," she said. "It seems to have a lot going for it. Maybe I should check out the job opportunities."

"I don't think the pay scale is very good," I said, eager to point out drawbacks to that idea. "It's mostly service industry here."

"Well, I don't need a lot to get along."

That was news to me. Mark always complained about her free spending.

I drove on up to Fourteenth Street and found Lottie's house, a modest bungalow with peeling white clapboard and badly faded shutters. Very little grass grew under the live oak tree that dominated the front yard, and a couple of scraggly bushes guarded the front door. As I began to get out of the car, Cindy grabbed my arm.

"I'm scared to sit out here alone," she said. "What if I get car-jacked or something?"

I should have known she'd be unwilling to wait in the car. I'm such a sucker. But I knew how she felt. So many horror stories are shown on television, we've all become paranoid.

"Okay," I said. "But I want you to sit quietly and not say a word. And I'm not going to explain to you what it's all about. Okay?"

"I'll agree to anything if you'll only let me go with you."

I knew I couldn't believe anything she said, but what could I do?

She followed meekly behind me as I went up to the front door, where a tall, large-boned woman answered my knock. Though she appeared to be about my age, she looked like she was from a different generation. Her clothes reminded me of the way my grandmother dressed when I was young: a button-front flowered housedress with no-nonsense, black, clunky, tie-up shoes and knee-high hose rolled down around her ankles. Lottie's hairstyle fit the role perfectly, with center part, marcelled waves, and bun at the nape of her neck. Even her glasses were sixty years out-of-date.

I introduced myself and Cindy, and she invited us in. The living room seemed the ideal setting for Lottie. Everything was straight out of the '30s, from the ugly brown sheared-velvet sofa and chair to the big wooden floor radio with the circular dial. I felt as if I were participating in time travel.

"Would you like some tea?" Lottie asked.

"No, thanks," I said. "We just finished lunch."

"Have a seat." She indicated the couch. "What can I do for you?"

When I called, I'd told her only that I urgently needed to discuss something with her. I hadn't gone into detail. "I understand you sued Rachel Greeson some years ago in small claims court."

Lottie looked astounded. "How on earth did you know that?"

"Those records are public. Anyone can look at them. It's even available through a personal computer now."

She put her finger to her lip thoughtfully. "Oh, I didn't realize that. Those computers. They're way over my head."

That didn't surprise me. Not that I should talk.

Cindy leaned forward. "Who's Rachel Greeson?"

I turned quickly and gave her a withering look, which she ignored.

"She's—" Lottie started to say.

I put my hand up. "Never mind. Cindy's not involved in this."

I was being bitchy, but I was furious at her. She sat back, hard, against the sofa, crossed her arms, and pouted. *Let her sulk,* I thought.

"I have a very important reason for asking," I said. "I know some-one who's looking for a baby-sitting job and has been interviewed by Rachel. When we researched her background and found out about the lawsuit, we wanted to know more about it. My friend thought the situation sounded ideal until this information turned up. So I told her I'd talk to you about it."

Lottie nodded. "There's no love lost between us. I don't mind answering your questions."

"When did you work for her?"

She thought for a moment. "It must have been five or six years ago. Her kids were two and three when I started."

"How long were you there?"

"About a year and a half, I think."

"What kind of employer was she?"

"She was kind of strange. She always hurried me out of the house before her husband came home. I never figured out why."

"What were the kids like?"

"Very shy. Frightened of their own shadow."

"Do you think they were abused?"

Cindy suddenly went into a spasm of coughing.

Lottie jumped up. "I'll get you a drink of water," she said and disappeared into the kitchen.

I started to hunt for a cough drop in my purse, but Cindy stopped coughing and leaned over and whispered in a frightened tone, "What's this all about?"

I wanted to strangle her. "I told you, Cindy. No questions. This does not pertain to you. Now, butt out."

She looked shocked that I spoke to her so sharply. Lottie came back with a glass of water, and Cindy drank it without another word.

"As I was saying about the kids," Lottie continued, "you brought up something that's been bothering me ever since I worked there. Little Chris—what a sweet boy he was—had a broken arm when I started working for them. He was only a couple of years old and, like I said, very shy. Rachel told me it was the fault of the last babysitter. But, you know, I was never real sure about that. Katie, who was three, talked like they loved her a lot and missed her. And they never mentioned their dad. It was like he didn't exist."

"They weren't separated, were they?" I asked. "Rachel and Harold?" If the children never mentioned him, and Lottie had never seen him, I wondered if Rachel had been hiding the fact that they didn't live together.

"No, because Rachel talked about him. She'd say things like 'Harold needs peace and quiet when he gets home. And he likes an immaculate house. Make sure the toys are all picked up and the kids are cleaned up before you leave.' He sounded like an uptight tyrant to me. But as I said, I never did meet him."

"Did you think the children were abused by him?"

Out of the corner of my eye, I saw Cindy's reaction. She shuddered and looked down at her hands clasped in her lap. I imagine things were hitting too close to home and she regretted begging to come in with me.

"I suspected it from the way they acted," Lottie answered. "Nervous. Not quite trusting me. A loud noise or quick movement would startle them far more than a normal child. They were extremely timid. But I had nothing of substance that I could report. No proof anyone was hurting them."

"Well, I appreciate your talking so openly about it," I said, standing up and preparing to leave.

Cindy stood too, anxious now to get out.

"I'll warn my friend against taking that job," I said.

"I think she'd be wise to turn it down," Lottie said as she walked us to the door. "I certainly regretted working there, and I'm sure Maria did too."

I stopped in my tracks. "Maria?"

"Yes, that was the name of the sitter who worked for them just before I did. The one Rachel said broke Chris's arm."

"Do you know her last name?"

"No. The kids called her Maria. That's all I know."

I was astounded. The day I had visited Maria Alvarado, with the board of Crafts From the Heart, she'd mentioned something about baby-sitting every chance she got. Maria was already linked to Gerry Stapleton with the embezzlement. Was she also linked to Rachel Greeson as their former baby-sitter? That seemed like an unbelievable coincidence.

CHAPTER · 14

CINDY FOLLOWED ME TO THE CAR LIKE A WELL-TRAINED DOG. MY mind was going a mile a minute, trying to place this new piece of information in its proper context. If, indeed, it had been Maria Alvarado who'd worked for Rachel, then could Rachel have been blackmailing her?

Everyone at Crafts From the Heart considered Maria above reproach. They'd all expressed shock when her embezzlement was exposed. And Lottie had said Rachel blamed Chris's broken arm on the baby-sitter. I wondered if Maria was taking money from the shop to pay off Rachel, who may have threatened to report her to the authorities.

Why would Rachel do that, though? I'd gathered from Reverend Packard that she had a hard time making ends meet. But the more I thought about it, the less likely blackmail seemed. The amount that Maria could get from the craft shop—probably two or three hundred dollars a month—wasn't enough to make a big difference in Rachel's lifestyle. That fact kind of took the steam out of my theory.

Maybe Helen Lawson, Maria's neighbor, knew something about Maria's baby-sitting history. I decided to drive to her condo and see if she was home.

"I'm going to visit someone else," I told Cindy as I started up the car, "and I'd appreciate it if you wouldn't interrupt us."

"I promise not to say a word," she said coldly. "After all, I'm just a nonperson here."

I'd begun to pull away from the curb, but I abruptly stopped the car. It was like someone had slapped my face—with good reason. I hadn't been treating Cindy with a whole lot of courtesy, having been mad at her practically since the day I met her. It now occurred to me, I'd never given her the benefit of the doubt. What an inopportune time to have such a flash of insight. I didn't have the time or patience to make up for my less-than-cordial behavior toward her.

"Look, Cindy, I'm sorry. I'm trying to do something for a friend, and I don't have time to go into details. I'm under a lot of pressure too. So forgive me if I'm short with you."

"Okay," she pouted. "Just remember, I have feelings too."

"I know." I tried to sound sympathetic.

During the drive to Helen's condo, I thought a lot about how I might develop a better relationship with Cindy. I hadn't done a very good job of it up so far.

We pulled up at Helen's, and I was relieved to find her at home. I didn't argue with Cindy this time about going inside with me, and I introduced her as my daughter-in-law because, technically, she still was.

"Helen," I said, "I hope you don't mind me bothering you again. But I keep learning new things that pique my curiosity."

"Don't mind a bit," she said. "I want to find out the truth about Maria. There are too many unanswered questions, and nothing adds up, as far as I'm concerned."

"Do you know if she ever baby-sat for Rachel Greeson? Back in the mid-nineties."

"Do you know the kids' names? She talked much more about the kids than she did the parents."

"Chris and Katie."

Helen thought for a moment. "Oh, yeah. I do remember those names."

"What did she tell you about them?"

"They were sweet little kids. She loved them a lot. Worried about them too."

"Did she tell you why?"

"She thought the parents didn't treat them well."

"Did she see any actual abuse?"

Helen shook her head. "No. It was more like they'd flinch if she raised her arm, as though they were afraid she'd hit them. They didn't act normal."

"Do you know why Maria left that job?"

A look of dawning realization came over Helen's face. "That's right. She told me they'd fired her and accused her of hurting their little boy. I'd forgotten about that."

"Do you think she really did that?"

"Are you kidding? Maria loved kids. Those kids, especially, because she worried so much about them. I remember she was devastated. Not so much that she lost her job, but because she wouldn't be around to make sure they were all right."

Cindy had been sitting silently the whole time, her mouth clamped shut in a grim line, as though she was afraid a word might inadvertently escape her lips. I could tell she was bursting to say something.

"Cindy?" I said, inviting her to join in.

"Why doesn't somebody do something for those kids? Are you telling me they're still with those awful parents?" Hers was the anguished voice of someone who knew firsthand about abuse.

"It looks to me like people have wanted to help them," I said, "but no one's been able to provide any proof."

"Nobody ever wants to get involved." Cindy's tone was bitter. "That's the problem."

"No. That's not true," Helen said emphatically. "I think Maria knew that if she went to the police, the parents would lay the blame on her."

"Do you think Rachel was blackmailing her?" I wanted to get Helen's take on the possibility.

"Holy moly! That could explain why she took the money from the shop, couldn't it?" Helen was becoming increasingly excited.

"If she didn't have a mother to send it to," I said, "and she obviously wasn't spending it on herself, where else would it go?"

Helen slapped her knee. "That's the best explanation I've heard. I think you're on the right track, Emma."

"What bothers me about the idea is that it couldn't have amounted to more than a few hundred dollars a month. That hardly seems worth the risk."

"Good point." Helen shrugged. "On the other hand, who knows what goes through people's heads when they do some of the idiotic things they do?"

"I don't suppose you have access to Maria's personal papers, do you?"

"No, 'fraid not. The police have been over there a lot. I imagine they've looked through all her stuff very carefully. If there was anything to indicate blackmail, I'm sure they would have found it."

Here I was again. A whole lot of speculation but no proof. I thanked Helen, and we left.

Cindy was quiet all the way to Siesta Key, preoccupied with her thoughts. She said little more until we were eating dinner.

"I sure wish we could help those kids," she said, laying her fork down after picking at her food and scarcely eating a bite.

Since she'd had no desire to have children while she was married to Mark, I was surprised at her growing concern over two children she'd never met. Perhaps experiencing abuse made her more sympathetic to anyone who'd suffered it. Maybe Cindy was gaining a little maturity.

"I wish we could, too." I not only wanted to help the kids, I wanted to know if my theory about Rachel and Maria was right. "But I don't know how to go about it," I said.

"Who else knows about this situation?"

"There's a girl from Rachel's church, Christie Anne. She's worried about the kids too, but she doesn't know enough to involve the authorities either. We've already talked about it."

"If she's a churchgoer, what about the pastor? Wouldn't he know?"

"I've talked to him. He said nothing at all to indicate he thought the children were in trouble."

"Couldn't you tell him what these two ladies told you today?"

"It's still only conjecture, Cindy. And this pastor . . . well, he's in such bad shape physically, I don't think he'd be up to doing much investigating."

She pushed her plate aside and lay her head on her crossed arms on the table. Her shoulders heaved as she cried silently. Her behavior was so unlike her usual aloof indifference that it shocked me.

I put my arm around her shoulder. "I'm sorry you're so upset. I'll try to think of something we can do." Though I hadn't a clue as to what that something would be, I hoped what I said would calm her.

We watched television the rest of the evening, since neither of us felt much like talking. My mind wasn't on the small screen, however; I couldn't tell you what show was on. We went to bed when the news came on at eleven, but I couldn't sleep because so many thoughts were running through my head.

I'd about exhausted all my resources trying to find out about Rachel. Those who were sympathetic to me had told me all they knew. I didn't dare keep questioning others like Tom Guy Packard, because I didn't know what their role was in the whole scenario. Bud and Arnold were much too scary to approach. If they didn't already suspect me of telling the police about their plan for the clinic, they surely would if I spoke with them. I didn't need to stir things up any more than I already had.

In the middle of the night, as I lay tossing and turning, I thought of one more person who might know something about Rachel. Clara McCarthy. The hospital was fairly large, but there was certainly a chance that they were acquainted.

However, the next day was Sunday, and I needed a break. I

decided that Cindy and I should do something fun. Feeling guilty over being so cross with her, I finally dozed off.

Cindy was still asleep when I called Cal at nine Sunday morning. "Want to go to Myakka Park today?" I asked him.

Myakka River State Park, east of Sarasota, once was the ranch of Bertha Palmer. She had also developed Spanish Point, where Cal had hurt his ankle. One of Florida's oldest and largest state parks, it features groves of live oak, a small lake, and acres of palmetto and indigenous plants. The park teems with wildlife, from alligators to turkey buzzards to an occasional sandhill crane. You can take an airboat ride around the lake to see alligators sunning themselves on the muddy shores—the airboat is necessary because of the water hyacinths that choke the local lakes and rivers. Or you can take a tram tour in open cars on wheels through the wilderness, to catch a glimpse of deer and armadillos. It's a wonderful place to get away from the city traffic and crowds.

"Sure," he said. "Looks like it'll be a beautiful day. Take a picnic?"

"I'll throw something together. By the way, I have a visitor. She'll be coming too."

"Oh? Who's that?"

"Cindy. Mark's estranged wife."

"You're kidding."

"No, I'm not." I described all that had happened since Cindy called from Toledo in tears.

"You're a generous lady, Emma. You notice I didn't say 'sucker.' Most people wouldn't have done that under the circumstances."

"I'm not so sure about the generous part, Cal. I was pretty pissed off with her yesterday. I don't know how long I can take having her around. I thought maybe if you were along today, she wouldn't get to me quite so much."

"Is that supposed to be a compliment?"

I laughed. "Sure. It was rather backhanded, wasn't it? Of course, I want you for your charming self too."

"Well, in that case, I'm raring to go."

We set the time for eleven, and I told him I'd pick him up in my rental car. He hadn't planned on getting a rental until Monday.

Cindy got up around nine-thirty. When I asked if she wanted to go to the park with us, she replied, "I guess so," in a most half-hearted way. Briefly irritated, I decided it was pointless to expect any enthusiasm from her. She was a psychological mess at the time, and I didn't have the smarts or training to deal with it. I'd just have to muddle through.

I let her fix her own breakfast, figuring it would do her good to take care of her own needs. She carried coffee and toast into the living room, then dropped crumbs on my white carpet while reading the newspaper, which she had spread all over the place by the time she finished. I always keep it stacked neatly on the coffee table. She left her dirty plate and cup on an end table when she went to get dressed.

Damned if I was going to clean up after her. When she emerged from the bathroom in her T-shirt and jeans, I said, as calmly as I could, "The dishwasher isn't full. And the sweeper is in the coat closet."

With her mouth set in a tight line of reined-in anger, she carried her dishes to the kitchen and swept the floor. The paper remained in disarray, but I felt I'd won at least a partial victory. I wasn't going to push my luck. One day at a time. That was the ticket.

I made two roast beef sandwiches apiece for Cindy and Cal, and one for myself. Cindy looked so emaciated, I hoped she'd eat them both. I put in raw carrots and celery sticks to offset the bag of potato chips and chocolate chip cookies. And for good measure, I added three shiny red delicious apples. Since I had only large bottles of Coke, which wouldn't fit in the small cooler, I decided to stop by a convenience store and pick up a six-pack.

I was halfway out the door, thinking that Cindy was following me, when I noticed she was walking toward the bedroom.

"Where are you going?" I called after her.

"I just broke my fingernail," she said as she disappeared around the corner. "I've got to fix it."

"We're late, Cindy," I hollered, exasperated. "Cal's waiting for us."

She came back to the living room almost immediately, which surprised me since she usually did as she pleased. "Okay, okay, let's go."

If I kept on her case, I figured, I might get her to think about somebody besides herself.

It was about a quarter till eleven by the time we left. I drove toward the northern bridge and met heavy traffic heading the other way, toward the shore. I knew it would be packed on Siesta and Turtle Beaches and was glad to be going the opposite direction.

Stopping at the convenience store at the corner of Siesta Drive and Orange Street, I picked up some cold Cokes and a *New York Times* we could read after our picnic. The store was busy, and I had to wait in line to pay, feeling cross with myself that I hadn't allowed more time to get to Cal's house. I knew he wouldn't say anything if we were late, but I have this thing about being on time.

After paying for the drinks and paper, I returned to the car. Before I even got to the driver side door, I noticed Cindy wasn't in the passenger seat. The girl was going to drive me round the bend. What on earth was she thinking? Had she wandered in the other door of the store to buy something, and we'd missed each other? *She's worse than a damned kid,* I thought. It was almost eleven o'clock.

I hurried back into the store and checked every aisle, but there was no sign of Cindy. I saw a wall phone but had to get back in line to get change so I could call Cal.

He answered almost immediately.

"It looks like we're going to be late," I said. "I stopped to get some Cokes, and Cindy's wandered off somewhere. I'd like to wring her neck. I guess I'll just have to wait for her in the car till she decides to come back. I hope it won't be too long."

"No problem," said Cal blandly, making me wish I could be as easygoing as he always is. "I'll be waiting for you. Turn on the car radio and relax. Don't let her ruin your day."

"Easier said than done."

Very much out of sorts, I went back to the car. I couldn't understand how Cindy could be so inconsiderate. When I opened the door, I saw a piece of paper lying on the passenger seat. What was she doing, playing follow the trail? I sat down quickly and picked up the sheet of notebook paper, folded in half.

I unfolded it and read the child-like printing in pencil: "We have your friend. If you want her back, you must do what we say. Do not call anybody. We are watching you every minute."

My immediate reaction was a rush of renewed guilt that I'd been so angry at Cindy. Then, as I realized the gravity of the situation, nausea swept over me, and a thrill of fear coursed through every nerve.

I prayed that, since I didn't get in my car after discovering Cindy gone, whoever took her realized that I hadn't read the note before I called Cal. Otherwise, they might have thought I was calling for help.

Looking around the parking lot, I saw several cars and SUVs, two or three of them with someone sitting in the driver's seat. Many of the vehicles had dark tinted glass, so I couldn't tell whether Cindy was in the backseat of one of them. Someone must have followed us from La Hacienda and had seen an opportunity to grab her while I was inside the store. If I'd been clever and alert, I suppose I would have noticed a car trailing me. But since Siesta Drive is the only way to get off the northern part of the island, it wouldn't be at all strange to have someone behind you the entire way.

I continued reading the note: "You must drive direct to Tamiami Trail and go south. A mile south of Osprey you will see a dirt road going east. There is an Exxon station on the corner. Turn down that road and drive till it dead-ends. We will be following you, so you better not try to pull a fast one."

It took me several minutes to get a grip on my panic. I fervently wished for a cell phone, although I knew that the kidnappers would see me using it. I remembered visiting Lottie Turnbull, when Cindy was afraid to stay alone in the car. I wondered if she was prescient.

I briefly considered sitting there, doing nothing. After all, we were parked near a main street, with customers continually going in and out of the store. What could her captors do? But it soon dawned on me that they could pull out at any time, taking Cindy with them, and I would never know. I couldn't let that happen.

With extreme reluctance, I pulled slowly out of the lot and headed down Siesta Drive to Tamiami Trail. A huge black SUV followed me, and I assumed it was the kidnappers till it turned off at the next block. Right behind it was an old green Chevy with its side windows tinted.

I could see in my rearview mirror that the driver had a floppy-brimmed fishing hat pulled low over his forehead and wore enormous dark glasses. His shirt collar was pulled up so it obscured the lower part of his face, making it impossible to tell if it was someone I knew. I was damned sorry Florida doesn't have front license plates, though I had to wonder if I'd ever have the chance to use them to identify anybody, anyway.

I turned south on the highway, hoping that I'd see a cop along the way and could somehow alert him. As if they're ever there when you need them. I drove slowly, trying to postpone the inevitable, past the retail areas along 41, past Sarasota Square Mall and the strip malls that had grown up around it, out into the more rural area. I drove by Spanish Point and the elegant residential areas that lie behind high grassy berms hiding the mansions from the proletariat driving by.

The green Chevy stayed about five car lengths back. I drove through the tacky business district of Osprey, with its run-down, flea-market-type buildings, a patch of "cracker" Florida juxtaposed against the wealthy "modern" Florida.

Before long, I spotted the Exxon station at the corner of the unpaved road. My mouth felt like someone had swabbed it out with a towel soaked in bile, and my hands clutched the steering wheel so fiercely, I wondered if I'd ever be able to pry them loose.

All along the way, I kept telling myself that somebody would rescue us, since that's the way it happens in movies. Of course, I knew that possibility was extremely remote. I couldn't believe we were going out into the wilderness to some unknown and probably horrific end.

I put on my left-turn indicator and veered onto the rutted road. The other car followed close behind. I drove slowly, my rental car bouncing crazily over deep potholes. This road was definitely not used often. It wound through wild growth as jungly as Siesta Key. The thick greenery that I loved so on the island was menacing here, shutting out the sunlight and promising nothing but danger.

CHAPTER · 15

AFTER ABOUT A MILE, THE ROAD—NOW ONLY A NARROW, RUGGED path—ended in a rough, rutted circle in a tangle of heavy undergrowth and live oak. I stopped, and the other car stopped twenty yards behind me. I sat there, unsure what to do next.

Suddenly, both rear doors of the Chevy opened simultaneously, and two men emerged, their faces contorted and unrecognizable under pantyhose masks. They both wore dirty overalls over dirtier T-shirts. One dragged Cindy from the rear seat, her hands tied behind her. The driver remained in the car, too far away for me to clearly see his features. Cindy was gamely twisting and turning, trying to get loose as they dragged her toward me, one on each side of her, grasping her upper arms.

I got out of the car, knowing I was helpless to rescue her, but there was no sense in letting them manhandle me out of my car too. I thought it best to put on as brave a front as I could, though I knew my face must be gray with fear, to say nothing of the rampant perspiration that stained my blouse. When I'm scared, I sweat like a stevedore.

The man on Cindy's right let go of her and strode toward me. She took that opportunity to try to wrest her arm away from the other man, but he tightened his grip so harshly that she cried out and was forced to her knees.

I felt like a sitting duck. I knew it was useless to flee; I couldn't outrun the six-foot-tall man. And even if I could make a break, I couldn't leave Cindy. Whatever help I might eventually muster would be far too late to rescue her. She'd either be dead or gone.

"What the hell do you think you're doing?" I demanded as he approached me, figuring that confrontation was better than cowering surrender.

He said nothing. Instead, he grabbed my left arm and twisted it behind me as I screeched in pain. It was only then that I noticed rope, as heavy as a clothesline, stuffed in his overalls pocket. He grabbed my other arm and roughly tied my hands behind me. It felt like wire cutting into my wrists. I couldn't see what he was doing, but I felt him cut the rope, so I knew he had some kind of knife. That didn't improve my state of mind, at all.

He swung me around, and I saw Cindy being dragged toward me.

"You stupid sons of bitches," I screamed, madder than hell now. "Can't you pick on someone your own size? Are you such weenies you have to pick on women?"

With that, my tormentor hauled off and slapped me, hard, across the cheek. My head snapped back, and I was briefly stunned by the assault. Mouthing off was going to get me nothing but agony, that was obvious. I'd wanted to goad him into talking, in hopes I'd recognize his voice, but he had sense enough to keep his mouth shut. In fact, both of them did.

Although my cheek was stinging from his blow, I couldn't help but think what a ludicrous situation we were in with those strange-looking creatures. In a feeble attempt to take my mind off our terrible situation, I began to think of my captor as "Mr. Potato Head."

With each of the men "escorting" us, grabbing our upper arms tightly, they half dragged us through the jungle for a mile or more. The cabbagy smell of the abundant foliage was strong, and the rustling in the undergrowth made my skin crawl. I'm not an intrepid outdoors person. I like my adventures tame.

The terrain seemed to get more rugged, the farther we went. I tripped a couple of times on tree roots, only to be hauled unceremoniously to my feet with such brute force, I thought Mr. Potato Head would dislocate my shoulder. I watched my steps more carefully after that, but I could barely keep up with his long strides.

Instead of wearing my usual sneakers, I'd worn sandals. Not a wise choice. I'd also worn shorts—something I seldom do—and I was paying the price. Though I tried to be stoic, every once in a while, when I stumbled or scraped my bare legs on something sharp or prickly, I let out a whimper. I could hear muffled sobs now and then from Cindy, too.

Finally, deep in the jungle, Mr. Potato Head stopped. The other man did too, jerking Cindy up short. God knew what lurked in the overgrown thickets: bobcats? Poisonous snakes? Fire ants? Alligators, if we were near water? I didn't want to think about it.

Without warning, I was thrown to the ground, and my tormentor began lashing my feet together. I struggled, but I had little strength left. Cindy was tied up too, and it appeared to me that she had given up entirely. She lay there passively as the other man wound the rope around and around her ankles.

Wordlessly, the two men finished their job and walked briskly away in the direction of the cars. In only a matter of seconds they disappeared into the dense foliage. I wondered how they'd find their way back, but they could have been experienced woodsmen. It was then that I realized I'd left my keys in the ignition. All along, I'd been entertaining the unlikely notion that someone would find our abandoned car and come looking for us. But now I was almost sure our abductors would take the car and dispose of it somewhere far away.

What a damn fool you are, I thought. *How can you even think of being found? You're never going to be able to untie yourself. You're either going to get killed by some animal or snake, or you're going to die from exposure and starvation—take your pick.*

Cindy was lying on the ground as if in a stupor. She hadn't moved or said a word since they'd left.

"Cindy?" I said softly, hoping she hadn't gone over the edge and become catatonic.

She turned her head to look at me. "Why are they doing this?" she said in a little-girl voice. "I haven't done anything."

"Unfortunately, you came to visit me," I said. "Someone's been trying to get at me for the past several days. I'm so stupid. I thought I would be safe if I was careful."

She looked at me mournfully. "If I'm going to die here, can you at least explain why?"

I told her I didn't want her to even think about dying. "We're going to get out of here. Believe it!" I said with as much vehemence as I could muster. It was hard to sound confident when I actually felt so little hope. Then I went back to the beginning and told her the whole story—as far as I knew it, anyway.

"So do you think those were the guys from the church? What were their names?"

"Arnold and Bud. I couldn't tell if it was them or not. Their faces were too distorted by the stockings, and I can't remember how tall they were when I met them because they were always on a ladder or the roof of the house we were fixing up. It may have been them. If they'd only talked, I think I would have known their voices."

"Not that it matters." She sounded morose again.

I wanted desperately to shake her. "Stop that, Cindy, right this minute. We'll never get out if you're going to give up. Tell me how they got you in their car." I had to keep her talking, or she'd slip back into a state of utter defeat.

"I was just sitting there, and they pulled up right beside your car. When there was no one in the parking lot, one guy jumped out, opened my door—damn, I wish I'd had it locked—and grabbed me and stuffed me in the backseat. He had a pocketknife, and he told me he'd cut me if I hollered. The other one tied me up, and the driver moved the car to the other end of the parking lot."

"Did you get a good look at the driver?"

"No, he never turned around. All I could see in the rearview mirror was the hat pulled down over his forehead, and his shades. Couldn't even tell what color his hair was. And he never spoke, either."

"Well, we can worry about all that later," I said. "Right now, we have to figure out how to get out of this mess."

Cindy looked at me hopefully. "Do you think we could scoot our way back to the road?"

"If we had six weeks or so. We'd have to scoot all the way to 41 before anyone would find us."

"Oh," she said, and hope faded quickly from her eyes.

"We've got to figure out some way to cut these ropes."

"I think it's impossible. They're so tight on my wrists, I think it's cut off the circulation. My hands are going numb."

"They weren't the most gentle people I've ever met," I said. "But what can you expect from Mr. Potato Head?"

"What?" Cindy looked at me like I'd lost my mind.

"Didn't you ever have that toy when you were a kid? I swear, those guys looked like him, with those stupid stockings on their heads. All they needed were googly eyes and big ears."

A slight grin crossed Cindy's face. "Yeah, they were pretty goofy-looking, weren't they?"

I hoped I could keep her in that state of mind. "What we need now is a trained squirrel or chipmunk who knows how to chew off ropes. Have you seen any lately?"

"Oh, come on, Emma. Don't be ridiculous."

I'd overestimated my ability to keep her entertained. I was pretty pitiful as a comedienne. She'd sunk back into her blue funk.

"Let's put our thinking caps on." I was serious now. "There's just got to be a way."

"Yeah, right," said Cindy. "Maybe hell's going to freeze over too."

"Cindy, for Pete's sake, snap out of your defeatist attitude. That's getting us nowhere."

She looked chastised. "I'm sorry."

We both remained quiet for several minutes as we thought about our plight. Quite frankly, it seemed more hopeless by the minute.

I managed to scoot myself to a nearby pine tree, where I placed my back against its trunk. I tried rubbing my arms against the rough bark in the faint hope of fraying the rope, but after two passes, I realized I was just scraping the skin off my arms.

The spiky leaves of a nearby palmetto plant gave me an idea. "Cindy, did you by any chance bring along a nail file for your broken nail?" I asked. Knowing how vain she was about all things pertaining to her appearance—or at least, she used to be—I couldn't imagine her not doing something about it.

"Oh, good grief!" she replied, so excited she startled a nearby thrasher, who flew up clattering from the underbrush. "I'd forgotten all about it. It's in my pocket."

"Which one?"

"The right side."

"Sit up," I commanded. I scooted over beside her and backed up to her side till my tied hands were next to her pocket. "Now, sit still while I dig for it."

It was hard to work my fingers into her pocket. Cindy liked to wear her pants tight, and there was little room for maneuvering. Evidently the file had worked its way down to the bottom of the pocket, and I couldn't reach it because of the bend at her hip.

"We're going to have to do it lying down," I said.

We lay down, back to back, and I instructed her to roll this way or that till I could wiggle my fingers into the pocket. It was hard to delve into it very deep with my hands tied together. I finally managed to push the bonds up an inch or two, which allowed me access to the bottom but cut off the blood supply to my hands. Just as my fingers were about to go completely numb, I managed to grasp the file between my first and second fingers. I drew it up slowly until it caught on the hem and slipped from my grasp.

"Oh, hell," I sputtered, utterly frustrated.

"What's wrong?" asked Cindy, who had patiently endured my probing fingers.

"The damn thing slipped out of my fingers."

"You almost had it, didn't you? You'll get it yet."

So the roles had reversed, and Cindy was now cheerleader.

I had to push the rope down my wrist and let the blood recirculate in my fingers before I could go on. After a couple of minutes, I had feeling back, and I began again. It took several attempts to get hold of it, but I caught the file between my middle and ring fingers, and carefully maneuvered it past the hem. As I pulled it free, it slipped from my fingers and fell into the underbrush.

"Well, this time I dropped it on the ground," I grumbled. "What a klutz."

"I'll get it," Cindy said, sitting up quickly and searching for it. She spotted it near my hip and scooted over to pick it up. "Come on," she said cheerfully. "Let me see if I can cut your ropes."

I inched my way over to Cindy and proffered my hands to her. She began sawing away with great enthusiasm. It was very awkward, having to do it behind her back with her hands tied, and since she couldn't see what she was doing, she occasionally managed to jab me pretty good. I stifled my cries of pain. I didn't want to dampen her zeal.

She sawed and sawed, but nothing much seemed to be happening. After fifteen minutes, she twisted around to look at the ropes. "Aw, I've barely made a dent in them. We'll never be able to do this."

"Have they been cut into at all?"

"Just a little bit."

"Then we'll take turns. I'll cut on yours for a while, then we'll switch back again. If we do it long enough, we're bound to succeed eventually."

"I doubt it," she said despondently. "But what the hell. We haven't anything better to do."

She transferred the nail file to me, and I began to saw on her ropes. After a few minutes, I said, "You know, this would go faster if we sang. How about a few rounds of 'Row, Row, Row Your Boat'?"

"That's silly."

"Do it anyway!" I ordered.

"Okay," she answered meekly.

And so we sawed and sang, trading off every fifteen minutes or so. We'd feel the ropes very carefully to find the place we'd been working on, so we wouldn't cut randomly. It was extremely slow going. My fingers got so sore and tired from working in such an awkward position and having to grasp the file so tightly, I thought they'd fall off.

After about an hour, Cindy said, "I've got to take a break. I can't keep this up."

"Let's rest for ten minutes, then," I said. "I know you want to get out of here before dark."

The thought of being there, bound, after dark, was about the most terrifying thing I could imagine. That spurred me on to feats of endurance I never thought possible. Evidently the suggestion had an equal effect upon Cindy.

"I'll take five," she said.

At least we were able to measure time. She could read my watch, and I could read hers. That let us know approximately how much time we had before the sun went down. In October, it set somewhere around seven, and we took our break about two in the afternoon.

The problem was, even if we could manage to cut through the ropes, I wasn't at all sure we could find our way out of the jungle. But I didn't want to tell Cindy.

Before long, she was suggesting songs we might sing. It's under the most dire circumstances that you discover the genuine individual beneath all the accumulated baggage. I was beginning to have hope for Cindy. She was coming through in the clutch.

An hour later, we were down to "sixty-five bottles of beer on the wall" when I felt the ropes loosen.

"You've done it!" I cried. "You've cut through."

"Oh, thank God." I could hear a catch in her voice.

With a lot of tugging and pulling, I was able to wrest my hands free of my bonds. I looked at my wrists. They were raw and bloody and sore. I went at the knot at my ankles, but since it had been tied so many times and pulled so tight, I couldn't get it undone.

"Let me have the file," I said. "Maybe I can use the point of it to loosen the knot."

Cindy waited patiently while I prodded and poked and dug at the knot. I figured I could free her more easily if both my hands and feet were unbound.

Finally I managed to untie the ropes. I flung them away in a fit of jubilation and went to work on Cindy. I was still a way from cutting through her ropes—evidence, I guess, of my lack of strength. So I pried her knot free with the file. When I got it undone, she tackled the one at her ankles and undid it in far less time than I had.

I decided right then and there to do some strength training at the local health club. That's how optimistic I was that I would get home. And that's how it went: optimism one minute, despair the next. But despair won most of the rounds.

CHAPTER · 16

"SO, WHICH WAY DO WE GO?" ASKED CINDY, NOW THAT OUR HANDS and feet were free.

I'd tried very hard to remember some tree or plant that would indicate the way we'd been dragged into the jungle. I'd seen movies about trackers, and hoped we could find our way out by following broken twigs and disturbed ground cover.

But Florida's lush greenery doesn't cooperate. Instead of brittle twigs and dried leaves, you have living plants that merely spring back after you've pushed them aside. I'm sure trained trackers could follow a trail, but I didn't have a clue.

"I think we came by that palm tree over there," I said. "We need to go west, so the thing to do is try to walk toward the sun." Since we'd turned left off 41 toward the east at the Exxon station, I knew we had to head back in the opposite direction.

"But you can hardly see it, it's so freakin' dark in here."

And she was right. The trees, especially the live oaks, formed a canopy of leaves that let little light through. But we'd just have to wing it. We had no other choice. We began to pick our way through the jungle, trying our best to remember whether anything seemed familiar to us.

"See that weird tree trunk there?" I said. "I'm sure we passed it on our way in." I wasn't at all sure, but I was clutching at straws. It seemed at least *slightly* familiar.

"I don't remember it."

"You were probably watching your feet at the time. I had to do that a lot to keep from tripping." I said that so she wouldn't be discouraged. My sinking spirits told me that any resemblance to trees we'd passed previously was strictly in my mind.

"I was concentrating on wishing the jerk dead. He was hurting my arm something awful."

"Listen, Cindy, we're going to see to it that those guys pay for what they did to us. The charge of kidnaping can put them away for life, you know."

She looked at me with a grim smile. "That thought is exactly what keeps me going. I plan to make damn sure they rot in jail."

We walked in silence for a long time, neither of us feeling up to chitchat. My wrists throbbed from the rope burns, my legs were cramping, and the mosquitoes wouldn't leave me alone. Every few minutes, Cindy would slap her arms or head and curse under her breath, so I guess they found her equally tasty.

Peering through the dark canopy of forest, we kept trying to locate the elusive sun.

All of a sudden, Cindy stopped. "Oh, no!" she wailed.

"What's the matter?" I couldn't imagine what upset her so.

"Look over there!" She was in tears now. "There's our ropes. We've been walking in a circle!"

Sure enough, the tattered remains of the ropes that bound us lay under the loblolly pine to our right. We had wasted almost an hour and had gotten nowhere.

I took hold of her arm to calm her, and she cried out in pain. I hadn't noticed before how badly bruised it was where she'd been dragged by our captors.

"Sorry," I said. "Look, Cindy, we can't panic now. That would be the worst thing we could do. We have to keep our wits about us."

She wiped her eyes with the back of her hand. "You're right, Emma. We can't get those bastards if we don't get out of here. Those potato heads are all I'm going to think about now. They're going to end up *mashed* potatoes before I'm through with them." So she'd maintained at least a smidgen of a sense of humor.

"As long as we're back here," I said, "let's take the ropes with us. They might come in handy somewhere." I began to pick them up and secure them around my waist.

Cindy picked two up and wrapped them loosely around her neck a couple of times, with the ends hanging down in front. "The newest fashion in necklaces," she said. "I might start a trend here."

The sun had been overhead earlier, making it almost impossible to gauge the direction we were going, but now it was lower in the sky. Though heavy growth still obscured it much of the time, an occasional opening in the canopy gave us a chance to reorient ourselves to the west, and I felt more confident. If we just kept heading toward it, we would have to come upon Route 41 sooner or later.

We picked up our speed a little, prodded by the frightening aspect of spending a night in the jungle. Again I mentally lambasted myself for wearing sandals and shorts. My legs were really a mess now, scratched and bleeding. I prayed I hadn't been rolling in poison oak or ivy.

Cindy, slightly behind me, let out a scream. I wheeled around to see her frozen in fear as a dark brown snake coiled to strike her. Its wide-open mouth revealed a white lining, and I recognized it as a poisonous cottonmouth. Before either of us could react, it struck her leg with lightning speed.

I saw a good-sized dead branch lying in the underbrush, and I grabbed it and brought it down with all the force I could muster on the snake's back. I pounded it and pounded it, far longer than necessary, turning the snake into a limp and bloody mess.

Cindy hadn't yet moved, immobile from shock. I led her to a nearby fallen tree and sat her down.

"Pull up your pants leg," I said.

"I can't. It's too tight."

"Then stand up and drop your britches."

She meekly did as she was told, untying her shoes with shaking hands and taking them off first so she could step out of her jeans completely. I examined her leg from top to bottom.

"The denim must have been thick enough," I said. "I don't see a mark on you."

She sank down to the dead tree in relief and put her jeans back on. Her face was still pale from fright, and she had difficulty fastening the snap at the waist. Her whole body trembled as she realized how close she'd come to disaster.

"You're one hell of a lucky girl," I said.

"I am," she said humbly. "I surely am."

All I could think of was my vulnerable bare legs and feet. If I'd been a tad slower, the cottonmouth would have bitten me. And I'd heard they were quite deadly. If nothing else gave me impetus to get out of the jungle, that three-foot-long piece of dead meat did.

I moved at a slow trot now. Under any other circumstances, I would have been too weary to even move, let alone hurry, but my survival instincts apparently had released incredible amounts of adrenaline. The trees seemed to be growing less dense, which was good news, but the sun was setting too quickly for comfort.

Cindy and I took turns leading the way, our eyes glued to the ground for predators when we weren't taking glances to make sure we were heading for the setting sun. I carried a large stick in my hand, just in case we ran into any more snakes.

But hurry as we did, we still had not reached the road by the time the sun was just above the horizon. I knew we had no more than twenty minutes, at most, before it became pitch black. I wondered if we should continue on in hopes we'd reach our goal during that half hour. Or should we prepare ourselves for spending the night there?

My heart opted for the first, but my head insisted preparation was necessary. Could I convince Cindy of that?

I was ahead, and I slowed down till she caught up with me. "We're running out of time," I said. "It'll be dark soon. I think we need to prepare to stay the night."

Her eyes grew wide. "Tell me you're joking."

"We have to face reality, Cindy. We don't have any way to make a fire, but we could clear a space for ourselves. There might be enough moonlight to see a little bit."

She closed her eyes and shuddered. My reaction exactly.

I found a space as much out in the open as possible. But *open* meant only that the overhead canopy wasn't solid; the vegetation on the ground was. I began by pulling up plants and tossing them aside. I wanted some bare ground, the way country people in the South had dirt yards they swept clean to keep snakes from sneaking up on them.

After some hesitation, Cindy joined in, and we created a circle about ten feet in diameter, free of undergrowth. I took off a sandal and tamped and smoothed the dirt. Seeing the pile of leaves I'd thrown aside gave me an idea. I selected the largest of the leaves and wrapped them around my legs and feet, securing them with the rope I'd salvaged. They would not only give me some warmth overnight, they might protect me from bites if any creatures wanted a taste of me.

The sun had set, and darkness enveloped us like a shroud. The shimmering heat of the day had cooled noticeably, and my sweaty clothes clung like a clammy swimsuit in a cool breeze. I started to shake uncontrollably.

Cindy and I sat back-to-back in the middle of the circle, each of us wielding sticks. I suggested we take turns keeping watch so that we might get a little rest. We probably wouldn't be able to fall asleep—we were far too terrified for that—but if we could close our eyes and rest in shifts, we'd have more strength in the morning.

We agreed on an hour each, and I took the first watch. Cindy crossed her arms on her knees and lay her weary head down. Once we'd quit talking, I was more aware of the many sounds of the night: owls hooting and eerie rustling in the undergrowth and overhead in the canopy of trees. As every nerve in my body seemed to buzz with fear, I felt like I'd been plugged into a light socket.

A little moonlight managed to filter through the opening in the leaves, but it only served to make shadows that were almost more menacing than complete darkness, especially when they moved. I held my stick at the ready to bash whatever wandered into our dirt circle. A tiny mouse skittered through during that first hour, but I didn't have the heart to kill it.

A few hours later, in the middle of the night, Cindy screamed. I'd halfway dozed off in that uncomfortable position, unable to fight my weariness any longer.

My eyes flew open as she hollered, "Look over there, by that tree." The moon had risen directly above us, giving us more light than before. She was pointing to my left, and I could just make out a roundish form at the edge of our circle. Then I realized what it was.

"That's an armadillo, Cindy. It's probably far more scared of us. It won't hurt you."

His bony armored body reflected the moonlight as he scampered away in alarm.

"I've never seen one before," she said. "What a strange animal."

To calm her down, I decided to share a little trivia. "If you see one on the road and try to pass over it, it'll jump up and kill itself on the underside of your car."

"Well," she said, "that'll be useful information when I get on 'Jeopardy.'"

"You'd better share your winnings with me, then."

After we'd exhausted our capacity for chitchat, I tried unsuccessfully to go back to sleep. I gave up and told Cindy she could rest and I'd stay awake.

The night dragged on as though it were unending. Every minute seemed stretched to infinity. The fact that I had a watch on with a face that lit up made it even worse, for every time I glanced at it, I was devastated to see how little time had actually passed.

Finally I saw the tiniest bit of light in the sky. I squinted at my watch and saw that it was six-thirty. We'd made it through the night without the world coming to an end.

Cindy stirred and lifted her head. She'd been sleeping for a while, something I'd been unable to accomplish. I felt as if I'd been awake and performing continuous aerobics for a week, my exhaustion reaching ever-new heights. I wanted to tell her to go ahead and make it to safety and bring someone back to get me. But, of course, I wouldn't do that. I'd never admit I'd let myself get so out of shape.

"Man, I'm thirsty," she said, stretching her arms over her head. "What I wouldn't give for a glass of orange juice and a huge cream-filled doughnut right now."

"You can have your doughnut. What I have visions of is a big pot of coffee. Fresh and hot. I sure miss my caffeine fix. Oh, well, I guess we ought to keep a lookout for water in a hollow stump, or caught up in some leaves. It's rained recently, so there ought to be some around." I sighed. "Why didn't my mother send me to Girl Scout camp so I could learn survival skills?" I muttered.

"My mom did, but I got so homesick, they had to call her to come get me the third day. I never went back. I didn't want to do all those dumb things like build a fire or sleep in a bag on the ground. Last night, I'd have given my eyeteeth for a sleeping bag or a fire."

I unwound the ropes from the leaves around my legs, tied them around my waist, and struggled wearily to my feet. My joints were so stiff, they nearly squeaked.

Now that it was morning, we would be walking away from the sun, not toward it. That meant we'd have to constantly check behind us to see if we were going west. I didn't have a lot of faith in our ability to do that, but what alternative did we have?

We'd been walking for an hour or so when we found a boggy spot where water had collected in low stumps and hollowed-out places in logs. I was so thirsty, the fact that it had unidentifiable little "things" floating in it did not give me pause. I scooped some up with my hands from a stump, while Cindy knelt down and drank directly from a log.

It wasn't till I'd partially slaked my thirst that I realized I hadn't seen this bog before. I could only hope we were close and parallel to the route we'd taken the day before. I made a vow to myself that I would buy a small compass and carry it at all times from now on.

"Look," Cindy said, pointing to our right. "There's some mushrooms. I'm starved."

"Unless you can tell which are poisonous and which are safe, I wouldn't risk it, if I were you."

"How about berries? Can we look for berries?"

"If we're still here five days from now, I guess we could chance it. But it's not even been twenty-four hours, Cindy. You aren't going to die of starvation anytime soon."

She held her stomach with both hands. "Wanna bet?" Then she smiled briefly. "Mark always said I'd eat him out of house and home."

That was the first time she'd mentioned Mark since the day she arrived. I couldn't help but wonder what was going on in her mind now when she thought of him.

We decided to take up our singing again. We could pace ourselves by it, and it did make the time pass a little faster.

We were singing "Danny Boy" when I saw the brightness in the distance. Dropping the song mid-verse, I ran toward the light and burst out into the clearing.

We'd made it to the highway! And toward my right, about a half mile or so away, I could see a tall sign stretching into the sky. It was the Exxon station, the one at the corner of the dirt road where we'd turned off 41 the day before.

Getting rescued now seemed a piece of cake. All we had to do was make it to the Exxon station and call Cal to come get us.

We were so elated, we walked down the shoulder of the highway arm in arm, like schoolgirls. I remembered how, twenty-four hours earlier, I'd been totally disgusted with Cindy. In fact, in all the years I'd known her, I'd thought of her more as my adversary than friend. Now you would have thought she was my best buddy.

I realized that I owed my life to Cindy. If it hadn't been for her and her nail file, I would still be lying in the woods, bound hand and foot. And there wasn't a doubt in my mind that I would have died there.

We laughed and joked as we walked down the berm. I felt as giddy as if I'd had three beers. We talked about what we would eat for our first meal—she wanted Chinese, and I wanted a hamburger and french fries—and how we couldn't wait to get in a shower. Grungy didn't begin to describe us.

When we were a couple of hundred yards away from the station, I stopped in my tracks for a minute, just to savor the sight. No sunset over Crescent Beach could compare to the beauty of that sign at that moment.

"Let's go," urged Cindy, sprinting down the road.

But before I could catch up to her, a sharp stinging sensation spread over my legs. I looked down in surprise and saw dozens of tiny ants swarming over them. I'd stepped right on a nest of fire ants! They're so tiny, you don't notice them until they decide to bite, usually in unison. I yelled and stomped my feet and frantically brushed them off with both hands.

Cindy turned around and came back toward me. "What's wrong?"

"Fire ants," I gasped in fear. "I've been stung before, and I'm allergic. Let's run for it."

She grabbed my hand, and we dashed for the station. As we burst in the door, a couple of customers and a clerk turned to look at us in alarm; I'm sure we were a sight to behold. I began to feel light-headed and strange, and sensed that my lips were swelling.

As I struggled to catch my breath and started to wheeze, Cindy screamed, "Call 911. She's been stung by fire ants!"

"Lady, the EMS is up the road a piece," said one of the customers. "It'll take them a while to get here. Why don't you let me take you to them, and they can meet us halfway?"

In spite of the terrible ordeal we'd endured at the hands of strangers, I nodded in agreement. I was sure I would die if we didn't accept his offer. We'd have to trust him.

As he helped me out to his car, the clerk called the dispatcher to alert the EMS to watch for us in a car with its emergency lights on.

CHAPTER · 17

I HAVE ONLY SCRAPS OF MEMORY ABOUT THE RIDE, BECAUSE I'D BEEN concentrating on trying not to panic or pass out. I was helped out to an old clunker of a car, where I fell into the backseat. Cindy jumped in beside me. I could feel my throat swelling, and my pulse was so rapid, I wondered if my heart would burst.

As we sped away, Cindy grasped my hand and kept repeating, "Hang in there, Emma, you're going to be all right."

All I could think of was what a strange twist of fate it would be to survive our kidnaping, only to succumb to ant stings just as we were about to make it home.

The car swayed as it flew up Highway 41, and I vaguely wondered if we might die in a car crash before we ever made it to the rescue squad. How many times could I cheat death? I hoped to hell that, like a cat, I had nine lives.

Breathing became more and more difficult. Cindy's face began to fade as she bent over me, willing me to hang on.

Suddenly the car swerved and stopped, with a great screeching of tires.

Cindy said in my ear, "We've met the ambulance. They'll take you the rest of the way."

As if at a great distance, I heard a door open and slam shut. Within half a minute, Cindy was gone and a man materialized next to me.

"I'm giving you a shot of epinephrine," he said. "That will help your breathing."

He could have been an archangel, as far as I was concerned. I tried desperately to fight off the darkness enveloping me. But it was a losing battle.

I was dimly aware that an ambulance had pulled up beside our car, and I felt several hands gently lift me out of the backseat and onto a gurney, which was then loaded into the back of the vehicle. As the siren began wailing and we sped off, someone poked at the bend of my elbow, while something shadowy hung swaying above my head.

The rest of the trip remains a blur, and I have only hazy recollections of being in the emergency room. By the time I began to be aware of my surroundings, I'd already been moved upstairs to a regular room.

"We're keeping you overnight for observation," the doctor said.

The swelling around my lips had gone down, and I could breathe a lot easier. But my legs were itching so much, I thought I'd lose my mind. When I pulled down the sheet, I saw they were covered with red bumps with infected pustules in the center. I'd had bad cases of poison ivy when I was a kid, but nothing compared to the tormenting itch caused by the fire ants. And all the scratches and abrasions I'd gotten in the woods competed for attention. But their pain seemed like a minor counterpoint to the agony of the stings.

I heard a knock on the door, then it opened, and Cal and Cindy burst into the room. Cal rushed to my side and picked up my hands in his, holding them so tight, I thought he'd crush them.

"Oh, Emma," he said, "I've been out of my mind, ever since you didn't show up yesterday. With all that's happened lately, I knew something was wrong. I called the police within the hour. They didn't get too excited until I got hold of Caronis, and of course he realized you might be in deep trouble. They've had half the force out looking for you. In fact, he's out in the hall now, but I asked him to give us a few minutes together first."

I smiled up at Cal. His kind face was the best medicine I could possibly have. "How did Cindy get hold of you? I never told her your full name or where you lived."

Cindy, who'd been standing back, came forward. "I called the police from the emergency room, and they called Cal. But neither of us knows how to get in touch with Mark."

"Do we have to tell him?" I pleaded.

"Yes," insisted Cal. "He'd never forgive us if we didn't."

"He works at a place called Little River Technology. In Tampa. Kind of go lightly, will you?"

"Lightly?" Cal seemed astonished. "You almost died, and you want me to go lightly?"

"You know how he is. Or maybe you don't."

"He tends to freak out," offered Cindy.

"I'll tell him what happened and try not to sensationalize it. 'Your mom went camping overnight in the woods. Had a little trouble finding her way out, but she finally got to the highway. Had a little run-in with some ants. But she's fine.' How's that?" Cal looked at me with a wry smile.

"Perfect. Keep it short and sweet."

"Caronis wants to talk with you, and then you need to rest. You'll probably get released tomorrow, and I'll come get you. In the meantime, I invited Cindy to spend the night at my house."

"Thanks, Cal. That's very thoughtful of you." I was relieved that she had someone to stay with. Of course, I didn't have a key to my house. Anyway, I didn't want her to be alone. Particularly not there.

As soon as they left, Detective Caronis came in. He picked up a chair and placed it next to the bed. "How are you feeling?"

"I'm starved. And I think I'll go mad from the itching of the ant stings. Otherwise, just great."

He smiled and nodded. "Right. Your daughter-in-law has filled me in pretty thoroughly. But I thought you might be able to give me some details that she may have overlooked. Why don't you start from the beginning and tell it from your point of view."

I tried to think of every small thing that might be helpful, but I couldn't be certain of much, except how frightened I'd been.

"So you can't identify your kidnappers?"

"I'd like to say it was Arnold and Bud wearing the stockings over their heads, but their features were too distorted. And they never uttered a word."

"What about the driver?"

"Between his hat and dark glasses, it was impossible to get a good look at him."

"Did you get a license number?"

"They were always behind me. Never could see the plate." I described the car as best I could.

"Your daughter-in-law gave us that information, but it's probably not enough to go on without the license plate number. We did find your rental car in a no-parking zone downtown. There were too many prints, from all the times it's been rented out, to be helpful."

"Shoot."

"I'd like to suggest that you not go home when you get out of the hospital. Until we get this solved."

"Don't you suppose they think I'm lying dead in the woods? Or at least dying?"

"They might stake out your place for a while, just to make sure you don't come back."

"I can't even pick up some clothes?"

"I wouldn't advise it. We don't want them to know you're okay."

"You know, of course, my purse was in the car with my checkbook and all my credit cards."

"One piece of good luck there. Your purse was thrown in the trunk. Unfortunately, they must have been wearing gloves. We only found your prints on it."

"How could you possibly know they were mine?"

"The condo manager let us in your place so we could get your prints for comparison."

I don't know why that bothered me so. It made me feel like I was the criminal. Nothing seemed sacred anymore.

"Anyway," Caronis continued, "they'd taken all the cash but left everything else. Probably figured it would be too easy to find them if they tried to use your cards. We kept the purse to go over for trace evidence, but I've got your cards and checkbook here for you. We also had your door lock changed, since we figured they had your keys. The new keys are in here too." He picked up a large manila envelope off the floor, where he'd put it when he came in the room, and laid it on my bed.

"Well, at least I can go buy some clothes now."

Caronis smiled. "Aren't you ladies always looking for an excuse to do that?"

I grimaced at the implicit sexism of his remark but said nothing. What would be the point of making a snotty reply? And I knew he was just trying to be cute.

He rose to leave. When he got to the door, he turned back and said, "If anything occurs to you that you haven't told me, give me a call. And let me know where you're staying."

"Okay," I said glumly. I wondered how long I would be banned from my condo. I was homesick for it already.

Exhaustion overcame me, and I fell asleep, in spite of the intense itching of my legs.

A couple of hours later, someone brought me a meal. I didn't know which I wanted to do more, sleep or eat. But eating won out. Even the plate of bland hospital food looked like a feast to me. As I finished my dessert of strawberry Jell-O, Mark came into the room, looking unstrung.

He sat in the chair by the bed and asked, "Are you okay?"

That was the most subdued response I'd gotten from him since he came to Florida. Somehow, I didn't think it meant he wasn't upset. Rather the opposite: he was like a potential volcano waiting to erupt.

"Yes, honey, I'm okay." I clenched my teeth, trying to endure the itching. I wouldn't let on.

"How could this have happened? Was it because Cindy was here?

I always knew she was a walking disaster. That woman is a magnet for trouble."

I hitched myself up in bed and bent forward to stare him in the eye. "You look here, Mark Daniels. If it weren't for Cindy, I'd be dead right now!"

He reared back, startled. "Cindy?"

"Damn right. She just happened to get caught up in a situation over which she had no control. And without the nail file she had in her pocket, I'd still be lying out in the jungle and never would have made it home."

"Oh," he said meekly. "I didn't know."

"Well, you'd better appreciate what she's done. Because she saved your old ma's life."

"Where is she?"

"She's staying with Cal. The police didn't want her in the condo till after they figure out who's responsible and get them in custody."

"What about you?" he asked. "What are you going to do?"

"They say they're going to discharge me tomorrow. I'll get a motel room."

"You promise you won't go back to La Hacienda till this is over." He had the look of a stern parent lecturing a kid.

"Okay, Mark, we've been down this road before. No ultimatums from you, please."

"You didn't listen when I said you should take taxis after the bomb was put in your car. And look what happened."

"Yeah. They probably would have kidnaped me and the taxi driver. And I'll bet he wouldn't have had a nail file." I smiled broadly, just to get his goat. He hated it when I gave some silly retort to his solemn statements.

After going over my story once again, this time skipping the worst of it, I convinced Mark that I was fine and he should go back to Tampa. I told him I'd let him know where I was staying, and he gave me the address of the apartment he'd just rented. His phone wouldn't be installed until Thursday.

Then I convinced a nurse I needed something for the itching, and she reached the doctor, who prescribed an injection. After getting some relief, I drifted back to sleep and didn't wake again until morning.

Cal arrived at my bedside by nine, even though the doctor hadn't discharged me yet.

"I want you to come stay with me," he declared, while finishing up the sausage patty I didn't want. I wondered how he could eat it stone-cold.

"I can't," I said. In my suspicious state of mind, I wasn't sure if he was simply concerned for my comfort, or if he wanted me there where he could keep an eye on me and keep me out of trouble. "You only have that single guest bed, and Cindy's already there. I can easily find a motel room, since it's not peak season."

"You can have my bed. I'll sleep on the couch."

"Huh-uh. I hate to say it, but that's about the most uncomfortable piece of furniture I ever sat on. You could never sleep on that."

He shook his head, his mouth a thin line of resignation. "You are a stubborn one."

I was discharged an hour later, with the doctor recommending I see my own physician about a therapy to immunize me against future ant stings. "You might not be so lucky next time," he warned.

The doctor left, and Cal surprised me with a bag full of clothes. He'd taken Cindy shopping the night before so she could buy some things to wear, and he had her pick out an outfit for me. She'd bought a pair of navy slacks and a red T-shirt, as well as underwear.

"She wasn't sure of your size, so I hope they fit," he said.

I was extremely grateful to have long pants, because it looked like I had smallpox on my lower extremities. Cindy hadn't been too far off, but I had to stuff some Kleenex in the bra because it was a cup size too big. Everything else fit fairly well. She hadn't thought to buy a purse, though, so I used the sack that the clothes came in.

The first place I had Cal take me was to a small older motel on the south end of Siesta Key, where I rented a room for a week. Thankfully, the rates didn't go up for tourist season until the end of the month, and I'd be near my beloved beach. The room had a double bed, so Cindy could stay with me if she wanted, and a tiny kitchenette with a sink, burners, and miniature refrigerator all combined in one unit. There was also a microwave oven and a television set, everything I could possibly need.

Then I asked Cal to drive me to a rental car company. "Better not make it the same one I used before. They might not want to rent to me again."

I drove away from the rental agency in a blue Chevy, after thanking Cal for schlepping me around, and headed for the bank and grocery store. I couldn't keep much in my little fridge, but I didn't want to eat all my meals out. I'd told Cal that I'd like to have a day alone, but if Cindy wanted to come stay with me the next day, that would be fine. It was up to her.

I went to T.J. Maxx and bought three sets of clothes, a purse, and a nightie. At Publix I picked up cosmetics and toiletries, along with a minimal amount of food. I couldn't believe how many little necessities one needs in order to carry on a simple existence. I imagined what families had to go through when their homes and belongings were destroyed by wind, flood, or fire. Our lives are filled with so many *things*. And we've become so dependent on them.

After cramming my perishables into the mini-fridge and storing the canned goods in the closet, I went out on the beach. Such a lovely sight. The day was calm and sunny, and the Gulf stretched like a great blue satin bedspread with a white lace flounce along the edge. It made me so nostalgic for my own home and bed, I was almost in tears.

Sitting on the sand on the towel I'd brought from the room, I tried to empty my mind of any thoughts relating to the past several days. Of course, that was impossible. And the more I thought about my experience, the angrier I got. I not only had endured great hardship, but now I was banned from my own home and the use of my own possessions. It was damned unfair!

I knew I'd have to leave the rounding up of the potato heads and their collaborator to the police, but if nothing else, I could at least talk to Clara McCarthy to see if she knew anything about Rachel Greeson. I decided to call her the following morning.

Just then it dawned on me that it was Tuesday, and I'd missed delivering Mobile Meals with Christie Anne. I hoped someone had taken over when they realized the meals hadn't been distributed. And poor Christie Anne must have been wondering what had happened to me. But since Caronis wanted me to keep a low profile, I decided I shouldn't try calling them with explanations and apologies. That would have to come later, after everything was cleared up.

When I went back to the room, the light was blinking on the telephone. Cindy had left a message to call her.

"How are you feeling?" she asked when I got through to her.

"Better. They gave me something for the itching."

"Well, a hot bath almost completely restored me. Is there anything I can do for you?"

I couldn't get over it. I don't think she'd ever asked me that before. "Don't think so. I have a double bed here at the motel. You're welcome to stay with me if you want to."

"Thanks. But I've never been very good at sleeping with someone else."

Of the female variety, I thought to myself.

"Cal has said I can stay here until we can get back into the condo," she said. "And I'm going to rent a car tomorrow and start job hunting."

I was so startled, I didn't know what to say. "Uh, okay, good," was all I could manage. "I'll talk to you soon."

So she was going to look for work in Sarasota. I wasn't sure how I felt about it. The first time she'd mentioned it, I'd been appalled. But things were different now. I'd developed some kind of bond with her, which is almost inevitable when you're thrown together with someone in a life-threatening situation.

I was still uncomfortable about the animosity between her and Mark. I hated being in the middle of that. But Cindy had changed. Temporarily, at least. She seemed less self-centered, more generous and thoughtful. Would it last?

CHAPTER · 18

I SLEPT WELL THAT NIGHT. I HADN'T GOTTEN MUCH REST IN THE hospital—the noise level, even in the wee hours, never improved much—so I fell asleep without having to count a single sheep. I felt renewed the next morning, both physically and mentally.

I prepared a breakfast of cereal and bananas but discovered, to my dismay, the coffeepot didn't work. I made a mental note to buy one, figuring it would probably take a day or two for the motel to replace it. And I wanted a cup of coffee ASAP. I can barely function without my morning dose of caffeine.

Then I called the oncology department at the hospital and asked to talk to Clara McCarthy.

"I know how busy you must be," I said after identifying myself. "Is there a good time to meet with you? I'd like to ask you a few questions."

"Oh, how is poor Mr. Stapleton?" she asked.

"It's been a few days since I've seen him, but he was about the same as he was in the hospital. I wonder if he'll ever get better."

"Poor dear. He has so many strikes against him."

She didn't know the half of it.

"He certainly does," I replied.

"What did you want to talk to me about?"

"Just some things relating to his welfare." I didn't want to get specific until I saw her.

"I don't know if I can help you, but I get a break about four this afternoon. Can you meet me in the cafeteria?"

"That'd be great. See you then."

I had hours to fill before I met with her. I hadn't seen Phil in almost a week, and he'd been asleep, so it really didn't count as a visit. It was time I reported back to Arlene on his condition. I wanted so much to be able to tell her he was improving. Almost as much as I wanted to tell her that her mother's murder had been solved. But after this long, I doubted I would ever be able to do either.

With that discouraging thought in mind, I drove to Brightwood Nursing Home. Tessie was at the nurses station as I passed by on my way to Phil's room.

"Miz Daniels," she hailed me. "I need to talk to you."

She hurried out from behind the desk and took my arm. "Let's go to the break room," she said, guiding me around the corner to a small room furnished with tables, chairs, and snack machines. We sat side by side on a small love seat, the only piece of upholstered furniture in the room.

"Is something wrong?" I asked. She looked quite grim. "Is Mr. Stapleton okay?"

"He's about the same. But something happened that you need to know about."

"What, Tessie?"

"Day before yesterday, someone sent him a box of chocolates in the mail. Poor dear, he's having trouble eating. He needs some work done on his teeth, and we're having to puree his food until he can see the dentist. But we didn't want to throw them expensive chocolates out. It seemed so wasteful. I'm trying to lose weight, so I didn't want to take them, but one of the aides took them home.

"She got real sick after she ate them," Tessie continued. "Upchucked all night. Course, she thought it was the flu. But I ain't so sure 'bout that. I think someone doctored them. And if Mr. Stapleton had eaten them, it probably would have killed him, he's so weak."

"Did you give the chocolates to the police so they could test them?"

"No. Ivory just throwed them out. Not because she thought they was poisoned or anything. But because after being so sick, she couldn't stand to look at them no more."

Oh, dear God, I thought. *Someone's going to get to Phil yet.* "What about the wrapping on the box? Was there a return address?" Not that I thought anyone would be stupid enough to do that.

"No, ma'am. I'm sure there wasn't. But it got throwed out, too, before Ivory got sick."

So there was nothing to check for evidence.

"Tessie, you're going to have to watch him like a hawk. I agree with you that someone was probably trying to hurt him."

Tears appeared in her eyes. "I'm trying so hard, Miz Daniels. I'll check any package what comes from now on. Even if it say it's from his daughter."

I leaned over and gave her a hug. "You're doing a grand job, Tessie. You're doing the best you can. Hang in there."

She walked me back to Phil's room. He was sitting in his wheelchair, and this time he was awake. He gave me a wan, lopsided smile, though I wasn't sure he remembered me. I talked with him for a while—or I should say *at* him, because he didn't respond, except for an occasional sigh or grunt. I touched only on innocuous subjects, like the weather or the birds outside his window on the feeder. It didn't take long to run out of safe things to say. So I sat for a while in silence, holding his hand. And he seemed to appreciate that. Sometimes a human touch can mean more than words.

Within half an hour, I was back in the car. Every time I visited Phil, I left in a quandary. Should I report to anyone about the candy? Definitely not Arlene.

I decided to tell Caronis. Unlike the accusing letter, this incident would prove that someone was trying to harm Phil, and that someone was surely the person who killed Geraldine.

* * *

Caronis was very solicitous when I was ushered into his office. He stood up, shook my hand, and claimed he was delighted to see me.

"How are you feeling now?" he asked.

"Much better, thanks. A good night's sleep does wonders."

"Have you thought of something you didn't tell me on Monday?"

"No. Nothing else has occurred to me about our abduction. But I wanted to tell you about Phil Stapleton. I just came from visiting him."

"How can I convince you to keep a low profile?" he asked, his tone accusatory. "I'd think you've been through enough already that you wouldn't want to take any more chances till we can find those perps."

"Look, Detective, I can't sit in a motel room forever. I'd go crazy. Besides, visiting a nursing home didn't strike me as being careless. Do you think they're staking it out, waiting for me to show up there? Disguised as a dementia patient, maybe?"

He smiled slightly, in spite of himself. "Okay, okay. I get your point. Just be careful."

"Of course. I'm not too keen on spending any more time out in the woods."

I then repeated what Tessie had told me. When I finished, he clasped his hands together, steeple-style, and looked at them thoughtfully for a minute or two.

"I wish I could tell you that was helpful," he said. "But without the candy or the box, there's no way we can know whether it was a poison or if the woman really had the flu."

"You don't think it seems awfully suspicious?" I asked.

He looked as though he wanted to say something encouraging to me but found it impossible. "I'm sorry, Emma. I think the chances are overwhelming that the woman ate something else that gave her food poisoning. Or she had a bad case of stomach flu. I hate to disappoint you."

Not half as much as I did. But I thanked him and left.

I went to the mall to buy myself a coffeepot and returned to the motel for a sandwich and a nice fresh cup of coffee. Then I sat on the beach, thinking positive thoughts, until it was time to go meet Clara at the hospital.

I felt this was my last chance to make some sense out of the past couple of weeks. If Clara could give me even the tiniest bit of information that could point to Rachel's involvement in either Maria's or Geraldine's deaths, I would continue to try to search for the truth. If not, there was nothing to do but acknowledge I had failed in my quest to help Arlene and Phil.

I found Clara sitting at a table in the hospital cafeteria, nibbling on a french fry smothered in ketchup, when I arrived at five minutes till four. An untouched sandwich was on her plate.

"Hi, Clara." I sat down across from her.

"Oh, Emma," she said, giving me her sweet smile. "How good to see you again."

We discussed the weather for a moment, a subject dear to the heart of most Floridians. Then she asked me about Phil. "You said he was doing about the same. Does he seem to be making the adjustment to the nursing home?"

"It's hard to tell, since he can't talk. It must be tremendously lonely for him, especially since he had to go there so soon after Geraldine's death."

Her expression turned sorrowful, and she shook her head. "It just breaks my heart. You said you wanted me to answer some questions. Since I specialize in oncology, I'm not sure I can be very helpful about his case. Stroke victims have such an unpredictable future. A lot depends on his attitude, which probably isn't very positive, considering what he's been through."

"I realize that. Actually, that isn't what I wanted to talk to you about, though there is some connection. I wanted to find out if you know Rachel Greeson. I understand she works in the housekeeping department here."

Clara's face turned a deep red. Her hand, which had been clutching an iced tea glass, began to shake noticeably. She suddenly put the glass down and placed her hand in her lap, her downcast eyes riveted on it as if it were some foreign object. I apparently had pushed one of her buttons.

"N-no, I don't believe I know her," she said in a shaky voice. "This place is pretty big, you know." She refused to look me in the eye.

I hadn't the slightest doubt that she was lying. For some reason, she didn't want to be connected to Rachel in any way. But what could I do? Call her a liar? Demand that she fess up?

Unfortunately, I couldn't prove that Clara knew her. So I changed the subject, and she recovered her poise as we chatted about nothing in particular. I was going to finish my coffee and get the hell out of there, my last hope dashed to pieces.

"Clara!" a harsh voice behind me demanded. "I need to see you now!"

I thought her supervisor had caught her still on break when she was supposed to be working. The speaker sounded very angry, and I turned in my seat to see who had such an imperious tone. I was absolutely floored to see Rachel Greeson.

Clara's mouth dropped open. She looked at Rachel in horror and then at me.

Rachel stared at me as though she might be trying to place me. We'd met only once, when we were cleaning Rose's house, and I'm not sure she knew my name, even then. If she's anything like I am, names are forgotten almost as soon as the introduction is over.

But Clara was obviously embarrassed to be caught up in a lie. "Excuse me," she mumbled as she rose from her seat, leaving her barely eaten meal to follow Rachel out the cafeteria door.

It was impossible now for Clara to deny knowing her. A lot of good it did me, since she'd left, but the hospital cafeteria was not the place to have a down and dirty argument with her, anyway. I'd find out where she lived and confront her there. Rachel had her thoroughly intimidated, and I intended to find out why. It couldn't have involved rank at the hospital, since Rachel was in the house-keeping department. How did she hold such sway over Clara?

I expected to have trouble finding out where Clara lived. But there her name was, big as life, in the telephone directory I borrowed from the receptionist's desk in the hospital lobby. She hadn't even bothered to use an initial instead of her full first name, as many women do.

Since I didn't know when she got off work and recalled that she visited her mother in a nursing home every day, I decided to camp out in my car near her house. On the way there, I visited a McDonald's drive-through window and got myself dinner, in case I had a long wait. Why do expediency and high cholesterol so often go together?

It was a couple hours later and nearly dusk, just as I was on the verge of giving up and leaving, that a Camry pulled into Clara's driveway. I decided to approach her before she got in the house, because once inside, she might not answer the door. I silently crept up to the rear passenger side so she wouldn't notice me. When she opened her car door, I rushed quickly around the car and blocked her way.

"Hello, Clara," I said.

She was so startled, she dropped her keys on the ground.

"What are you doing here?" Even in the waning light, I could tell she was pale and drawn.

"I want to talk some more. There are things you're not telling me."

"No, I'm too tired. I can't talk now."

I decided to pull a bluff. I had nothing to lose. "If you won't talk to me, I'm sure the police would be interested in interviewing you." I couldn't imagine what they would interview her about, but invoking the name of the police might scare her into talking about Rachel. There had to be something sinister going on there for Clara to deny she even knew her.

Without warning, she broke into intense sobbing. I didn't budge.

I intended to stand there until she told me why she'd always been cool and collected, except when I mention Rachel's name.

Her sobs gradually subsided. She inhaled a deep sigh that must have reached to the soles of her feet, and leaned over to pick up her keys. "You might as well come in," she said, her voice quavering with emotion.

Saying nothing, I followed her into the house. She threw her keys and purse onto a table in the foyer and led me into a small living room, where we sat side by side on a green sofa. A dim overhead light in the foyer provided the only illumination as we sat in the shadowy room. Either she didn't want to see the expression on my face, or she didn't want me to see hers.

She looked down at the carpet, her hands clenched tightly together in her lap. "I can't live with it another minute," she said, her voice now expressionless. "I'm tired of pretending everything's okay. I can't eat. I can't sleep. My job's in jeopardy because I can't concentrate. Not that it will matter after I tell you."

She paused, as if waiting for me to ask her what she meant. But I kept quiet, figuring she had a compulsive need to tell me, and it would be better to let it come out on its own.

"Rachel saw me do something, and my life has been hell ever since." She looked up at me, her eyes pleading for understanding. "There was a man on my floor, a man by the name of Spencer Brower. I've seen a lot of people die from cancer, but his was the worst case I've ever seen. His pain was intractable. Nothing seemed to alleviate it. He begged me for days to put him out of his misery. Finally I couldn't stand it anymore and decided to do what he'd asked. I waited till he was asleep, then I smothered him with a pillow." She began to cry again. "I really thought I was doing the right thing." She shook her head in despair.

Spencer was the elderly man who'd died the day before Geraldine. We'd all been certain it was a natural death. Now I discovered that his demise was a murder as well. It was as if a plague had descended upon our building.

I couldn't help but feel sorry for Clara. Her misery seemed to hover about her, tangible and grim. Almost without realizing it, I put my arm around her shoulder to comfort her. So much for my plan to be aloof. My gesture brought forth a torrent of words.

"Rachel happened into the room at that moment. She came in so quietly, I didn't see her till it was too late. I pleaded with her not to report me. I knew it would be the end of my career, to say nothing of jail. And my mother is in a nursing home with Alzheimer's. They are always short of staff, and I feel like I have to be there for her, do the things the staff can't do. And pay for some of the extras that Medicaid won't cover. She needs me." She broke down at the thought of what might happen if she couldn't oversee her mother's care, covering her face with her hands as she sobbed.

"So what did Rachel say?" I asked.

Clara fished in her pocket for a tissue, and carefully wiped away her tears. "She said she'd keep her mouth shut if I'd do something for her. That woman is the devil incarnate. She said there was another patient in the hospital that she wanted the same thing to happen to. When I asked her who it was, she said Geraldine Stapleton. I was dumbstruck. I knew she wasn't going to die soon, and I liked her a lot.

"I told Rachel I'd have to think about it," she continued. "But she was relentless. She harassed me all day at the hospital, then called me at home and said she was going to report me the next day if I didn't do it. I prayed to God over it, but I was so scared, and I didn't want to go to jail. I have to take care of my mother. So I gave in."

She looked up at me. I was so horrified, I couldn't think what to say. My horror must have shown in my face, because she quickly looked at the floor again.

"She's been blackmailing me ever since Spencer and Geraldine died. I have to give her a hundred dollars every month, or she says she's going to the police. She tried to get more out of me, but I told her I just didn't have it."

Blackmail! So Rachel must have been blackmailing Maria, too, threatening to report her as an abuser. And now Rachel was extorting money from Clara.

But neither woman could give her significant amounts. It seemed so pointless. I felt compelled to ask Clara if she knew why.

"Why blackmail you for just a hundred dollars a month? I don't get it."

"One of her coworkers once told me Rachel spends big bucks every month on lottery tickets. She says she knows she's going to win a bundle someday and quit her crappy job—her exact words—and enjoy life for a change."

So Rachel bought into the myth about becoming a millionaire through the lottery. She couldn't afford to use her household money for that many tickets, so she blackmailed Maria and Clara to pay for them. The woman had to be looney tunes.

"Did she ever tell you why she wanted Geraldine dead?"

Clara nodded glumly. "It's that church of hers. It's the most important thing in Rachel's life. She idolizes her pastor . . . what's his name? Reverend Stacker?"

"Tom Guy Packard."

"He must have them hypnotized or something. She practically worships the ground he walks on."

"I guess his parishioners find him irresistible."

"Rachel says Geraldine was responsible for a suit against the church. It cost them tens of thousands of dollars, and they've been struggling ever since. It's like she built it up in her mind until she got obsessed about getting even. And when she found out Mrs. Stapleton was in the hospital, she decided to get even in a big way."

As Clara talked, it was almost as if she'd forgotten the gravity of her acts. Perhaps she was emotionally transferring all the blame to Rachel.

I needed to bring her back to reality. "I've got to know this, Clara. How could you visit Phil in the hospital after what you'd done? I don't understand how you could face him."

Her expression turned remorseful. "Rachel said I had to keep an eye on him. She'd heard the police thought he'd killed Mrs. Stapleton, and she wanted to make sure he didn't regain his speech and convince them otherwise. She thought that since I'm a nurse, I'd have a better handle on his condition than she would. I've got to tell you that after that visit, I went to the restroom and lost my lunch."

"Did you try to harm him after he went to the nursing home?"

Her eyes were wide in surprise. "Oh, no! In fact, I tried to convince Rachel that Phil would never again be able to speak, so she shouldn't worry about him. I didn't know whether he would or not, but I was sickened by the whole thing. I couldn't stand the thought of anyone else being harmed."

"I assume, since you've told all this to me, you plan to repeat it to the police."

For a moment she looked shocked. Then her face crumpled again and she said simply, "I will. I can't live like this."

"Then let's go down to police headquarters right now."

She stood up. "I'm ready. Just let me freshen up before I go."

I waited impatiently in the foyer. The strain of the past few hours had taken its toll on me, and I wanted to get Clara to the police station and let the cops take over. But she didn't come.

After ten minutes, I began to have bad vibes about her. The house was eerily quiet. I didn't hear the sound of running water, or any other sound, for that matter. Could she have gone out a back way? Was she going to flee to avoid prosecution? I was alarmed, because without Clara's testimony, the police probably wouldn't believe me when I told them Phil didn't kill Geraldine. Nor would they have any evidence against Rachel.

I looked for the kitchen and checked the back door in the dim light from the entry hall, but it was still chained from the inside. I found my way down the hall to the bedrooms. A glow of light from the one at the back guided me toward it.

When I entered, I saw the bathroom door ajar, its light falling across a bed where, to my horror, Clara was sprawled, unconscious. Blood from her slit wrists stained the log-cabin quilt. I felt her carotid artery and could detect a faint pulse. Instead of having any compassion, I was furious at her. How could she do this? How could she leave poor Phil swinging in the wind?

Sick at heart, and fearing she would die before I could get help, I called 911. It seemed like déjà vu when the paramedics swarmed into the bedroom a short while later and began working over her. I had my prayers to God for recovery down pat now, I'd used them so many times. But this time had a little different twist to it: *Save this woman so she can save Phil.*

CHAPTER · 19

I WAS BACK IN MY OWN HOME THE NEXT DAY, SERVING DINNER TO Cindy and Cal, when Detective Caronis made a special trip to give us an update. He joined us at the table for dessert, apple pie a la mode. I'd been in such a good mood, I'd made it from scratch.

Caronis said it was touch and go for a while, but Clara pulled through. And, apparently, her brush with death made her appreciate life all the more. She told the police the whole story in exchange for a manslaughter charge, rather than first-degree murder.

All the pieces came together when the detectives interrogated Rachel. She admitted everything Clara had confessed to. Even though it was inadmissable in court, the threat of a lie-detector test intimidated her, and the fact that Clara would testify against her convinced her to talk. She also had the mistaken idea that since she'd not committed a murder with her own hands, she wouldn't be punished as severely, even though her court-appointed attorney tried to tell her otherwise. For a devious and deadly plotter, she didn't have many smarts. Her absolute belief she would win the lottery was clear evidence of that.

Bud and Arnold, her collaborators, were responsible for Maria's death. Rachel admitted she'd been blackmailing the former babysitter for an injury to her son that had actually been inflicted by his father. But she'd convinced Maria that she could coach the boy to testify against her. When Maria told Rachel the board of Crafts From the Heart had discovered she was embezzling from them and she could no longer pay her, Rachel was worried that the truth would all come out. She sent Bud and Arnold over to convince Maria that she should not reveal the real reason she'd been taking the money.

Rachel could always coerce the thugs to do her dirty work because they'd bragged of felonious acts in front of her. The men were supposed to simply scare Maria, but when they broke in, she pulled a pistol from her nightstand. They got overzealous trying to take it from her, accidentally killed her, and made it look as though she'd shot herself. They at least were smart enough to wipe off all their prints from the gun and elsewhere.

"What about Rachel's children?" I asked Caronis. "What's happened to them?"

"The Department of Children & Families picked them up this morning. They're being evaluated, and their father is under investigation for abuse."

"Thank God they're out of there. I hope it isn't too late."

He looked particularly solemn. "It's always too late, as far as I'm concerned. Those kids will be affected for life."

I thought about the pictures of his own children, lovingly displayed on his desk.

"So what about all the stuff I went through?" I asked.

Caronis confirmed that Bud and Arnold were also responsible for all the terror inflicted upon me, again at Rachel's request. They sent the fake bomb, placed the real one under my car, and—no surprise—were the potato heads of our abduction. They'd enlisted a friend to be the driver that day.

Rachel had sent the letter to the nursing home, accusing Phil of killing Gerry, as well as the poisoned candy. She'd also made the threatening calls to me and Cal. The pillow that had been found over Phil's face soon after he was admitted to Brightwood must have been an accident. No one took responsibility for that.

The police could not ascertain whether Reverend Packard had any significant role in all the mayhem or not. Rachel claimed he had no knowledge of her involvement in Gerry's death. She'd become so alarmed by his deteriorating health, she wanted to retaliate against Geraldine. In her mind, she'd become convinced that the lawsuit had triggered Tom Guy's health problems, which surfaced about the same time as the settlement. But whether he was involved was a moot point, since he'd just been admitted to the hospital in critical condition.

"We've got it all pretty well sewn up," Caronis told us. "Everyone involved couldn't wait to implicate each other. You'd think they were having a contest: Who Can Spill the Most Beans? It's almost laughable."

"Just so they're not running around loose," I said. "They're a bunch of clowns, but pretty deadly ones, at that."

"Don't worry. They're probably not going anywhere for a long, long time."

"Which brings up a question. I called Phil's daughter, Arlene, this morning and told her the good news. She wanted to know if she could transfer her father to a nursing home near her."

"Sure. No problem."

"So the police did insist that he stay in the area as long as he was under suspicion?"

"We wanted him in our jurisdiction in case he got better and we could question him. Hated to keep him away from his daughter, but under the circumstances, our hands were tied."

Exactly as I had suspected. I was sure Phil would be much happier when he could see Arlene and his granddaughter regularly.

"By the way, when do I get my car back?" I asked.

"Yeah, me too," chimed in Cal.

"We'll deliver them to you tomorrow. We've even had them washed and waxed for you." On that upbeat note, Caronis left.

The three of us sat around the table without saying a word for a while. I guess we were all thinking about the past couple of weeks and all we'd been through. I know I could scarcely believe that the terror was over, that I could go back to living a normal life again.

At last Cindy spoke. "It's been pure hell," she said and hesitated. Then she gave us a shy smile. "But what can I say? I sure do appreciate you guys a lot."

"Well, Cindy, I owe my life to you and that fingernail file. I hope you have it cast in bronze or something."

She reached inside the neckline of her T-shirt and pulled out the file. "I sewed a little pocket inside each of my bras," she said. "I never intend to be without this precious thing again." And she kissed it before returning it to its hiding place.

Cal and I looked at each other and howled with laughter. Just then the telephone rang.

"Hi, Mom, it's Mark. My telephone's finally been installed. I tried to call you at the motel, but they said you'd left. Does that mean everything's okay?"

"It's more than okay. Why don't you come down this weekend, and I'll tell you the whole, long story."

"So now I can quit worrying about you?"

"For a few hours, anyway."